OCTAVIA E. BUTLER

OCTAVIA E. BUTLER
THE LAST INTERVIEW
and OTHER CONVERSATIONS

with an introduction by SAMUEL R. DELANY

 MELVILLE HOUSE
BROOKLYN · LONDON

First Melville House printing: July 2023

Melville House Publishing   Suite 2000
46 John Street   and   16/18 Woodford Road
Brooklyn, NY 11201   London E7 0HA

mhpbooks.com
@melvillehouse

ISBN: 978-1-68589-105-3
ISBN: 978-1-68589-106-0 (EBOOK)

Printed in the United States of America
1   3   5   7   9   10   8   6   4   2

A catalog record for this book is available from the Library of Congress.

CONTENTS

INTRODUCTION

SAMUEL R. DELANY

The first I heard of Octavia Butler was when West Coast writer Harlan Ellison phoned me in New York to tell me there was going to be a student in Clarion he wanted me to pay special attention to. Her name was Octavia Butler, and at that point, it was a Clarion tradition that the previous week's instructor would phone the upcoming instructor and alert her or him to any particular problems among the 20-odd students that one should pay special attention to. When I got there, Butler was, first, the only black student in the class, and it was soon clear she was extremely smart but also pathologically shy. She never volunteered, but if you just called on her, she always had an intelligent answer that was right-on. A number of the other students, including two who were just a little bit younger than she was, Joe Manfradini and Jean Mark Gawron, personally I took to much more than I took to her, both of whom moved to New York where they became personal friends.

Some months later, I saw her story "Crossover," in the first Clarion anthology, which seemed to be basically a slice-of-life story about a young working girl. It's accurately observed but not memorable in any other way, and I did not see her again until 1991 when the new Schomburg building went up at 135th St and Malcolm X Boulevard, New York. As part of the first year's program, Octavia and I were asked to read together. She had not yet won her MacArthur. I had not seen her since Clarion, and, for me, she was very much a West Coast writer.

We weren't given an auditorium, but there was a reception connected with the event, and the woman who did the catering, Norma Jean Darden, was a kissing cousin of mine on my Aunt Virginia's side, whom I'd known since I was a child, visiting in Montclair, New Jersey. Toward the end of the reading, we got a black heckler, who had just come in off the street, and I was really astonished when Octavia stood up to him quite articulately and told him to keep quiet and not interrupt till, finally, he got up and left. This was not the pathologically shy young woman I remembered from Clarion, and I told her how much she had improved. Years later, in her essay, "Positive Obsession," I would read:

Shyness is shit.

It isn't cute or feminine or appealing. It's torment, and it's shit.

I spent a lot of my childhood and adolescence staring at the ground. It's a wonder I didn't become a geologist. I whispered. People were always saying, speak up, we can't hear you. I memorized required reports and poems for school, then cried my way out of having to recite. Some teachers condemned me for not studying. Some forgave me for not being very bright. Only a few saw my shyness. She's so backwards, some of my relatives said . . .

Octavia had conquered the shyness. Sometime later, when she realized that, like me, she was dyslexic, she ceased to do readings in public altogether and generally gave remarkably coherent and impressive talks. Decades later, in my first years at Temple University, she came to talk: it was five years beyond her MacArthur Award, and, thanks to it, she was one of the best-known writers in the country. I was asked to interview her, and in preparation, I had read her novel, *Kindred*, which had struck me as a very interesting novel about an interracial marriage between a black young woman and her white husband, with a time-traveling element about a white ancestor she had to keep alive in order to exist at all. The audience that had turned out to see her were largely black women students, and it was clearly an audience that she felt she had spoken to before in various parts of the country. When I brought up the interracial question, she rather sharply ignored that aspect and went back to what she was clearly used to saying for that audience. I wasn't going to push it, certainly, if there were aspects she and her audience were not necessarily going to be interested in that day.

It's one way to handle interviewers, but her playing so entirely to audience's expectations did surprise me. Using her stories and novels to educate audiences during a live appearance was not what she wanted to do—or at least not that particular sort of audience.

In April 1997—I just had a birthday—in Atlanta, I joined Steve Barnes, Tananarive Due, Jewel Gomez, and Butler for the first Black Science Fiction Writers Conference, and after the opening ceremonies, for some reason, someone decided, possibly because I was gay, they would send us to a hangar-sized Atlanta gay bar and park us there for the evening. All the others had things to do except Octavia and myself, and so we found ourselves sitting together in this huge party space with some very loud music, though we asked to be moved as far back as we possibly could because, basically, we wanted to talk, and up by the stage—I suspect it was a good New York city block away—it was far too noisy.

I only remember one point of the conversation, but I think it's important given what some people have said since then. Neither one of us was particularly a bar person, and I don't know where the notion a gay bar would be an advisable place to park the two of us came from, but possibly because it was a gay bar, I asked her, "Octavia, are you gay?"

She shrugged and said, "Probably," and we went on to chat about other things: largely the blooming romance that had been going on between Steve Barnes and Tananarive Due for the entire weekend.

I will say right now that "probably" is a pretty ambiguous answer to a straightforward question. I assume it meant it was something she had thought about enough times to return to it on several occasions but had very little experience of it. Then again, it was certainly not a "no."

Less well-documented, I remember a rainy night just outside Washington, D.C., in a program sponsored by the Smithsonian, where we met at the theater and shared some orange juice backstage before going on. During the program itself, I read some from my story, *Atlantis: Three Tales*, and Octavia simply gave a talk. One young man, during the Q&A afterwards, lining up at the microphone, asked whether she would read his film script that he had brought with him, and she simply said "no," for which she got points in my book. I have no idea whether this was recorded or not, but I suspect it was either the last time or one of the last times I saw her in person.

We were separated by a continent, and, between Harlem in the '40s and '50s and Pasadena, Los Angeles, in the middle '50s through the early '60s, life was simply different enough to mean we had extremely different childhoods. (I have no idea whether Butler ever learned to drive or not; I didn't, largely because I grew up and lived practically till I was 50 in a city that, between subways and buses, has one of the best public transportation systems in the world, which, in a word, is why neither I nor my sister—or my partner Dennis—ever bothered to learn.) It's impossible to find out from anything published so far whether she owned a car or possibly wanted one. There is one reference to her never learning to drive, which means, for someone living on the West Coast, something very different from someone living in New York City.

On November 18, 1996, Butler's mother died, and it was deeply disturbing to her. A year later, she wrote a letter to her agent Merrilee Heifetz, apologizing that *Parable of the Talents* would never be finished, and asking to return her advance. It's my suspicion that she was never really happy with the longer form of the novel. For me, her teachable and her inspiring work are her short stories, especially "Amnesty," at the tail end of her career, and "Bloodchild," at the opening, which she often talked about as her male pregnancy story. She rescued one old novel (*Fledgling*) from her trunk, which makes up her second-longest contribution to her Library of America volume.

I am very pleased that they chose to put all eight short stories, as well as five of her essays, in that commemorative volume. I really think that is the best of Octavia Butler that we are going to find in a volume of collected works and certainly the most informative volume in terms of what she thought and what she told the various people who interviewed her from 1979 to the beginning of 2006, a month before her death at the end of February when the last of the interviews here, with Jen Chau Fontán, occurred. Ms. Fontán writes, "Octavia Butler . . . describes herself as a fifty-eight-year-old writer who can remember being a ten-year-old writer and who expects someday to be an eighty-year-old writer." Tragically, Octavia died a month later, on February 24, from a brain bleed associated with a fall she took, returning to her own Seattle house, which, as I understood it, she had purchased to be nearer to the city's science fiction community.

—Philadelphia
June 12, 2023

OCTAVIA E. BUTLER

THRUST INTERVIEW

INTERVIEW BY JEFFREY ELLIOT
THRUST
SUMMER 1979

Like her characters, Octavia Butler is a survivor, a bright new talent who describes herself as "a dreamer, a loner." One who amused herself as a child by making up stories. Fortunately for science fiction readers, Ms. Butler is now writing stories for a much larger audience. In recent years, she has penned such impressive works as *Patternmaster*, *Mind of My Mind*, and *Survivor*. She is presently completing two new novels, *Keep Thee in All Thy Ways** and *Wild Seed*, both of which promise to elevate her to superstar status in the science fiction world.

The interview which follows was conducted at the author's home in Los Angeles, California.

JEFFREY ELLIOT: Why did you become a writer?

OCTAVIA BUTLER: I stumbled into writing when I was ten and in love with horses and living in the middle of a city where no horses were available. I read horse books from the library—*The Black Stallion*, *King of the Wind*, *Smokey*, etc. I dreamed of owning a horse and told myself horse stories. Then at a carnival I rode a weary ancient pony that had

---

*   An early working title for what would become *Kindred*.

sores on its sides and flies attacking the sores. The pony walked around a small ring with other ponies bearing other children. The children kicked the ponies' sides urging the animals to go faster than their handlers would permit, and I understood where my pony had gotten his sores. I went home repelled (thus began my hatred of all exhibits in which living animals are treated as toys, machines, or wax dummies) and began to tell myself stories of wild horses. These were much more exciting than my earlier stories and I began writing them down so that I wouldn't forget them. I didn't know that writing was a profession, that people were paid for creating books I enjoyed. I learned quickly, though, that I liked to write. It was something I could do alone, and I was a naturally solitary person. It was apparently not a sin as so many pleasurable things were in the fundamentalist beliefs of my mother's church. And it was a natural extension of my dreaming. When I did find out that there were people who earned their living as writers, I knew that was what I wanted to do. No other work interested me. No other work ever has.

ELLIOT: What encouragement did you receive from your family?

BUTLER: My family saw my writing as an unusual hobby, harmless but impractical. "Get training for a real job," they told me. "Write in your spare time." One of my aunts said she didn't believe a Black person could earn a living writing. She told me to get a civil service job that offered security and a reasonable pension when I retired. My mother thought I should be a secretary because secretaries were always needed and they made more money than she ever had as a maid. Security. My mother and my aunts and uncles had lived through the depression. They remembered hungry, jobless, desperate times. Thus, to them, even loathsome work that was secure was better than writing, which they regarded as a form of gambling. They were right about that last, of course. Writing is a form of gambling. Still, they never told me not to write, but only to be practical and not depend on writing for my living. Good advice. I ignored it, but it was good advice.

ELLIOT: Why did you turn to science fiction?

BUTLER: I graduated from horses to science fiction with the encouragement of a bad movie. I had read some science fiction before my "graduation." I sampled everything that looked interesting in my second home, the Pasadena Public Library. I had read a few Heinlein novels and some Winston juveniles. But it was the movie—*Devil Girl from Mars*—that reached me in just the right way to make me try my hand at writing science fiction. The movie was just bad enough to disgust me and make me believe that I could easily write a better story. I was twelve at the time and I produced a god-awful story, but it didn't matter. In the process, I discovered that I enjoyed writing science fiction, and so I put my horse stories away. I had a lively imagination and interests in astronomy and anthropology that seemed to fit together perfectly in science fiction. When I was thirteen, I submitted my first story—a story typed for me (but not corrected or altered in any way) by my favorite teacher—my science teacher. Not surprisingly, the story didn't sell, but I was hooked. I've been writing science fiction ever since.

ELLIOT: How did your background prepare you to write science fiction?

BUTLER: It didn't. I write science fiction because I love it, but I have no scientific background or education. In school, since the only writing major offered was journalism, I skipped around changing majors often, somehow managing to graduate with an associate of arts degree in history from Pasadena City College in 1968. I also attended California State University, Los Angeles where I took several classes in history, English and social science before I dropped out. My only preparation specifically for writing science fiction came in 1970 when I went to Clarion, Pennsylvania, for the Clarion Science Fiction Writers' [and Fantasy] Workshop. This was a six-week session of writing, criticizing, and being criticized. The teachers, one for each week, were Joanna Russ, Samuel R. Delany, Harlan Ellison (who was also my teacher here in Los Angeles at classes offered by the Screen Writers Guild), Fritz Leiber, Kate Wilhelm, and Damon Knight. The workshop's director, also a writer, was Robin Scott Wilson. The Clarion Workshop left Pennsylvania some time ago, but has continued in other states. It's the best writing class experience I've ever had and I recommend it to anyone who is serious about writing science fiction. *The Writer* and *Writer's Digest* magazines usually carry notification of where to write for information about it in their May issue.

ELLIOT: Which writers most influenced your development in the science fiction field?

BUTLER: No doubt a great many authors have influenced me in ways I'm not aware of—authors I was temporarily addicted to as I was growing up. A partial list includes Eric Frank Russell, J. T. McIntosh, A. E. van Vogt, Wilson Tucker, Edgar Pangborn, Robert Heinlein, Isaac Asimov, John Wyndham, John Brunner, Ray Bradbury, Fredric Brown, Arthur Clarke, etc., etc., etc. I read science fiction voraciously as soon as I turned fourteen and was allowed into the library's adult stacks where most of the science fiction was kept. And I wrote story after story with no idea of what my reading might be doing to my writing. Also, I discovered the science fiction magazines and read them whenever I could afford them. I had certain other author additions, however, that definitely affected my writing. First among them was Zenna Henderson whose People stories I read one by one in science fiction magazines and anthologies, then all together in her books, *Pilgrimage* and *No Different Flesh.* Her group of gentle, psionic aliens are no doubt literary ancestors to my own ungentle, all-too-human Patternists. Another author I deliberately allowed to influence me was Theodore Sturgeon, whose characters come alive in even the worst of his stories. Later, I came under the influence of Frank Herbert and Ursula Le Guin. I was attracted to them by the complete, detailed world they create in *Dune* and *The Dispossessed* respectively. When I'm desperate for something to read, I want a book that creates another world for me. In a lesser sense, every novel, science fiction or mainstream, does this. But for me, these two novels do it more smoothly, more believably than most. In mainstream, Mario Puzo's *The Godfather*, Elliott Arnold's *Blood Brother*, Chinua Achebe's *Things Fall Apart*, and James Clavell's *Shogun* place me in equally different, detailed "other worlds" populated by interesting, believably different characters. I find myself working toward writing this kind of large world-creating novel.

ELLIOT: Is there a salient theme or concept which underlies your work?

BUTLER: There is, although I never planned that there should be. I've written several times about people striving for power. In *Patternmaster* and *Mind of My Mind*, my main characters strive for power because without it they will be manipulated and molded in ways they cannot tolerate. In *Survivor*, the main character has knowledge and influence rather than power, but it amounts to the same thing. The character uses what she has to prevent her from being killed or controlled. Power fascinates me, at least partly because I have so little of it. And people fascinate me. What will they do with power? What will they allow it to do to them? How did they get it? How will they hold it—or lose it? What will it do to their relationships with others? Etc., etc., etc.

ELLIOT: Is there a particular picture of the world which you wish to convey in your writing?

BUTLER: Only the picture of a world, past, present, or future, that contains different races, sexes, and cultures. All too often in the past, science fiction writers made things easy for themselves by portraying a white, middle-class, male-dominated universe, even attributing white, middle-class, male values to their "alien" races. I'm not comfortable writing about such a universe, behaving as though it represented the one true way.

ELLIOT: Do you strive to have a conscious impact on your readers? If so, what impact?

BUTLER: First of all, I like to tell them a good story—take them to a world they haven't seen before, a world I've enjoyed creating and hope they'll enjoy inhabiting for a few hours. As I've said, I want to portray human variety. I want to do it, though, without lecturing or resorting to stereotypes, and without the kind of self-conscious writing that communicates discomfort or lack of familiarity with my subjects. I've run across these problems enough in other people's writing to want to avoid them in my own.

ELLIOT: Do you enjoy the actual process involved in writing?

BUTLER: I love it. I've heard other writers say they dislike writing, but enjoy having written. I love both.

ELLIOT: Do you have a favorite among your novels? If so, which one, and why?

BUTLER: Of my published books, *Mind of My Mind* is my favorite. It takes place today rather than in the future or

past. It occurs in a renamed and somewhat changed version
of my hometown, Pasadena. (I changed the city to make
it a little more like the Pasadena of my childhood and to
use a neighborhood that no longer exists.) *Mind*'s main
character begins as a combination of myself and my friends
of several years ago. The novel was easy to write, fun to
write, and parts of it paint vivid pictures. Of my novels
not yet published, my favorite is To Keep Thee in All Thy
Ways. This is the story of a modern Black woman thrust
back in time to early nineteenth-century Maryland. It's a
story I thought about and wrote fragments of for years,
but did not want to research. Researching slavery—and my
character is immediately enslaved—promised to be painful
and depressing. Writing such a novel promised to be even
more depressing. But the story would not leave me alone.
It wanted to be written. I began uncertainly, tentatively,
and finished my first market version still wondering what
I had produced. I sent it off to an agent who held it for six
months without showing it to anyone, then sent it back to
me. I reread it, saw that I did have a novel—a potentially
good one—and rewrote it. I got more involved in it, found
myself examining my own feelings about slavery—not
what it was like for my ancestors, but what it might be
like for me. How could slavery reshape her emotionally?
Would the compromises, the capitulations she would have
to make destroy her? If not, why not? I didn't have much
fun writing To Keep Thee in All Thy Ways, but I think it's
the best novel I've completed so far. It will be published
both as science fiction and as a mainstream novel in the
summer of 1979.

ELLIOT: Why do you shy away from strong, heroic figures, as opposed to more average, ordinary people?

BUTLER: My characters are often combinations of people I know or have met, or at least of people who have made me notice them somehow. I collect impressions of people in my notebooks and in my memory. Anyone who impresses me either negatively or positively could wind up contributing to the formation of my characters. I remember "collecting" a slightly deformed retarded* man I used to talk to at a bus stop in downtown Los Angeles, and I collected several ministers and a couple of traveling evangelists. There was an old woman who used to be a mentalist with a carnival. There were a couple of prostitutes. There were several tough, cunning women who had managed to survive and raise their children against terrible odds. On and on. People are fascinating—real people. My characters get into such unusual situations that it helps for them to be recognizably human. They might have strange abilities or strange afflictions, but they are people. I can care about them as I write about them and I hope readers care about them as they read my work. "Heroes," on the other hand, bore me. They are usually flat and predictable.

ELLIOT: Could you briefly contrast and compare the storyline and style of each of your three novels to date?

BUTLER: A recurrent theme of mine is the striving of trapped or enslaved people. Teray from *Patternmaster* strives only for

---

*   Editor's note: the word was not considered offensive in 1979.

freedom, but he achieves power as well. Mary in *Mind of My Mind* strives for power so that finally she can fulfill her own needs, but that power she achieves gives her control over a great many other people. In *Survivor*, Alanna is trapped between three different groups, lying carefully to each, playing them against each other, all in the hope of freeing her people. Clearly, I'm interested not just in power, but in powerless people gaining power. Also, in each of the three novels, my characters use whatever power they gain for the benefit of their people as well as for their own benefit. There is some idealism left in me, I suppose.

ELLIOT: If you were asked to assess your work, how would you do so?

BUTLER: I'm becoming a more careful writer. I tended to ignore stylistic flaws in my first three novels if the flaws seemed small. Now, everything is significant. Flaws might still get by me, but not because I've deliberately let them. I'm not a fast writer, and in the past, I've hesitated to take the time to rework a "pretty good" scene when I've thought of a way to make it better. Now, I force myself. The difference between my first market version of To Keep Thee in All Thy Ways and my revised market version convinced me that the time was well spent.

ELLIOT: Are you envious of the major science fiction writers who enjoy tremendous commercial success, particularly since you're in the process of establishing your marketability as a writer?

BUTLER: God, yes! But I learned long ago that for me, envy could be constructive. Successful science fiction writers are my goads, my examples, and in some cases, my friends. I want my work to succeed as theirs has, thus their success helps keep me working through my worst times. Their success proves to me that success is possible and precludes any excuses I might make to myself for not achieving it.

ELLIOT: Why are there so few Black science fiction writers or, for that matter, Black readers? Is the field hospitable to Black writers? Do they face any special problems?

BUTLER: When I sent *Patternmaster*, my first published novel, to Doubleday, the novel was all I sent—not information about my race. I've had writing teachers, especially in college, whose judgment I didn't trust because they seemed to have trouble dealing with my blackness. I was nearly always their only Black student. But I never worried when I sent out a novel. It may be more possible in writing than in any other profession to be judged on one's merits. A Black science fiction writer who writes about Blacks as well as whites might hear from a few startled fans who aren't used to prominent Black characters and who aren't comfortable with them. I've received a little of that. But beyond that, the only problems I've had have been with my friends and relatives who think science fiction is a waste of time, and who, before I began selling, urged me to "do something else." Black people striving to succeed, or merely to survive, may have little patience with something as "unreal," as "impractical," as science fiction. Of course, in many cases, the fiction such Blacks read is at least equally impractical and unrealistic, but it is not as likely to take place in an all-white universe. As I've said, science fiction writers make things easy for themselves by writing about the universe as though it were located in their neighborhood. That kind of universe can turn off people who live somewhere else—or even local people who don't care much for the "place" they've been relegated to. Women, I mean. Only recently have women begun coming into the field in large numbers, and by their writing, drawing other women in. Women tend to write about women characters as people rather than as stereotypes. Blacks are needed as writers to write about Blacks as people rather than as stereotypes or tokens. I suspect that *Star Trek*, *Star Wars*, and *Close Encounters of the Third Kind* have stimulated the interest of many Blacks—especially young people. Some of these people will probably go on to become science fiction readers as well as viewers, and some of the new readers will doubtless try writing. Science fiction writers come from the ranks of science fiction readers. While I was at Clarion, in 1970, I attended my first science fiction convention, PgHLANGE in Pittsburgh. I saw one other Black person at that con. Now, I've just come home from IguanaCon, the 36th World Science Fiction Convention. There were still few enough Black fans for us to notice each other with interest, but even allowing for the face that IguanaCon was much larger than that 1970 PgHLANGE, the increasing number of Black fans is indisputable. And for every fan with the will, the time, and the money to travel to a con, there are others who merely read and enjoy science fiction. I had been reading it for years before my PgHLANGE experience made me aware of fandom. There may be more Black science fiction readers than we think.

ELLIOT: You've described science fiction as "a genre by and for thinking, reasonably unprejudiced people." What did you mean?

BUTLER: Exactly that. Science fiction presents differences, alternatives. Alternative societies, technologies, philosophies, alternative species of intelligent beings. It requires people to use their imaginations, stretch their minds, think. It does not require them to display good judgment or great intelligence or, in fact, lack of prejudice. I think I overstated there. But somehow, I've always gotten along with even the most conservative science fiction readers and writers I've known—not to say I've liked them all or agreed with them, but we didn't shut each other out. There was room for conversation, argument, thought. We were people a little more than ordinarily accustomed to dealing with differences.

ELLIOT: How would you characterize the treatment of Blacks as story characters in science fiction?

BUTLER: Problem: since I've been earning my living mostly by writing, I haven't had that much time to read science fiction. For that reason, I don't feel as secure as I might about what I'm going to say. I know that most science fiction, at least until a few years ago, contained few Black characters. And in the comparatively small amount of science fiction I've read recently, Blacks are hardly represented at all. Has anything changed? Yes. Now, when Blacks are represented, they're not likely to be insulting stereotypes. However, some writers do wind up introducing Blacks only to sweep their blackness under the rug. That is, a writer may tell us a character is Black, but then proceed to write about him as though he were white or as though everyone around him were color-blind. This can be legitimate in writing about the distant future or about alien societies in which some other difference has eclipsed race. In my book, *Patternmaster*, for instance, there's a Black character whose color doesn't matter at all because her people judge each other solely on psionic strength and ability. But this kind of writing isn't legitimate when it deals with the present or the near future. No Black, especially in the United States, is likely to be permitted to forget he is Black.

ELLIOT: What explains the lack of strong women characters in science fiction? Is this problem being remedied?

BUTLER: American science fiction began as a genre by and for young men who were interested in science, technology, and various forms of high adventure. Women, when they appeared at all in such fiction, existed mostly to motivate and/ or reward male success. Such women were not often three-dimensional characters (and frankly, neither were the men). Very little was required of them by their creators or expected of them by their readers. As science and technology had been considered male preserves, science fiction also became a male preserve. Some women writers sold their work to science fiction markets, but usually by using neutral names, male pseudonyms, or their initials. Science fiction attracted women readers slowly since, like Blacks, women were not likely to find themselves realistically portrayed. Insulting stereotypes were the rule. But in recent years, women have been entering the field as readers and as writers in large numbers. I am, as far as I know, the only Black woman writer, but I don't expect to be alone for too long. I've recently met two other Black women who are struggling toward their first science fiction sale. More women writers have meant not only more realistic women characters created by women, but more realistic male and female characters by both men and women. Perhaps more realistic Black characters will encourage the creation of more realistic characters of all races.

ELLIOT: What are the salient problems which a newcomer, like yourself, faces when it comes to making it in the science fiction field?

BUTLER: Basically, a new writer faces five problems. First, getting a market quality manuscript finished. Second, getting it published. Third, getting paid. Fourth, surviving on what you're paid. Fifth, trying to write your way off this particular merry-go-round and into solvency. At last, I seem to be getting there. It's probably easier to sell a science fiction novel than it is to sell a mainstream novel. There is less competition and the market is growing. But there is also less money. I know people who are making a good living writing science fiction, but they are either very prolific or damn good business people or both.

ELLIOT: Finally, what are you working on now? How is it progressing?

BUTLER: I've already mentioned *To Keep Thee in All Thy*

Ways, the story about the Black woman transported back to
the antebellum South. I have a few revisions to make on it
quickly. Doubleday is in a hurry. Summer, 1979, isn't that far
away. I'm also working on *Wild Seed*, a novel in my Patternist
series. *Wild Seed* is peopled by characters taken from Igbo
mythology—an Onitsha woman shape-shifter and a stranger,
more spirit than flesh, who resembles the Igbo *ogbanje*, an evil
child-spirit that transmigrates from body to body, leaving a
mother with a series of dead children. Unlike the Igbo original,
my *ogbanje* continues his evil habits into adulthood. These
characters can also be seen in *Mind of My Mind* at a much
later stage of their lives. *Wild Seed* will also be published by
Doubleday. As for my other novels, right now, all three are
available in hardcover from Doubleday. *Mind of My Mind*
and *Patternmaster* are available in Avon paperback.

EQUALITY OPPORTUNITY FORUM INTERVIEW

INTERVIEW BY ROSALIE G. HARRISON
EQUAL OPPORTUNITY FORUM
1980

ROSALIE G. HARRISON: How did you become interested in science fiction (SF) writing?

OCTAVIA E. BUTLER: I have always read sci-fi. I enjoyed it when I was young although I didn't realize it was a separate genre. As a child I wrote many stories about horses; I was crazy about horses. One day, when I was twelve, I was writing one of my horse stories and watching television when I noticed that I was watching a really terrible science fiction movie. I thought, "I can do better than that." So, I turned off the TV and I wrote a SF story. Reading or watching a dreadful SF story has been the impetus for a lot of science fiction writers.

HARRISON: What were your early writing years like?

BUTLER: Frustrating. Frustrating. During those years, I collected lots of frustration and rejection slips.

HARRISON: What kept you writing despite the rejections slips and frustration?

BUTLER: People. People who were willing to listen to me

even when I was rolling in rejection slips . . . somebody who would listen and not say, "You're crazy; why don't you do something else?"

The people who have had the most influence on me are people that I've never met. Writers, mostly. They wrote books—corny self-help books. Not the seventies type which say, "Get them before they get you." I'm talking about books like *The Magic of Thinking Big*. They are incredibly corny, but they gave me the kind of push that I needed and that no-body among my family or friends could give me. These books helped give me the ability to persist. I would go and read them almost the way some people read the Bible. They would help me go on despite feelings of absolute worthlessness.

I had one very good teacher who is also a writer, Harlan Ellison. He gave me a lot of help and a hard push or two when I needed them. It so happens that he writes a lot of fantasy and science fiction and was able to give me the kind of help I wouldn't have received from some English teacher.

HARRISON: Will you ever work in other genres?

BUTLER: There's always going to be something a little strange about my books or characters. For instance, the novel *Kindred* did not come out of SF. It's fantasy. But that is probably as far as I'm going to get from SF.

Right now, I'm working on a novel about a woman who develops a cancer somewhere around her pituitary gland. She is very reluctant to have any kind of surgery because one of her relatives died in surgery and her father shot himself because he had cancer. So she lets it go and lets it go, and it slowly develops that she's growing a new gland. She is a kind of mutation.

HARRISON: What do you find most beneficial about writing science fiction?

BUTLER: The main benefit for me is the freedom. For instance, I'm planning a novel that will take place in ancient Egypt and it will have [the] Doro character from *Wild Seed* going back to his origins. I've written a novel that takes place in the distant future and one that [takes] place in the present. I have written two novels about early America—one in colonial times and one in pre-Civil War days. In SF you can go into any sociological or technological problem and extrapolate from there.

HARRISON: What sets sci-fi readers apart from the general reader?

BUTLER: I think science fiction readers are a little bit more willing to use their minds. They want different things to think about. They don't want to read about things as they are. They're bored with the present. Maybe they want to escape from the present. A lot of science fiction readers start out as the weird kid, the out kid in junior high or grade school. When I went to the Clarion Science Fiction [and Fantasy] Writers' Workshop, I was surprised to find myself surrounded by the out kids. People who are, or were, rejects. Science fiction in America began with a lot of young people, the weirdos, who were interested in science and technology.

Their interest in people was not always encouraged by their social circumstances.

HARRISON: Let's talk about the writers for a moment. How many successful Black writers are in science fiction?

BUTLER: I know of three who are actually living off their work. I'm one. Steve Barnes who also lives in LA is another. And Samuel R. Delany who lives in New York City is the third.

HARRISON: You're the only Black woman science fiction writer.

BUTLER: Yes. That's true. It makes me the smallest minority in science fiction. At this moment, at least.

HARRISON: Blacks don't seem to read a lot of science fiction. Why is that do you think?

BUTLER: I think it's a kind of circular problem. I think Blacks don't like to read about a universe that is either green or all-white.

HARRISON: What do you mean? Martians and white people?

BUTLER: You have your aliens, extraterrestrial beings, and white humans in most science fiction stories. I think the only way to remedy that is to have more Black science fiction writers. Unfortunately, SF writers [come] from SF readers, and since not very many Blacks have been attracted to SF, we have very few Black science fiction writers.

At my first SF convention in 1970 there was one other Black person there. I went to a convention in Boston this year and there were a large number of Black people. I do not see a slow growth in the Black SF readership.

HARRISON: Science fiction movies have been big box office hits in the last two or three years. The big one, *Star Wars*, excluded minorities, but in the sequel, *The Empire Strikes Back*, Billy Dee Williams is one of the main characters. Do you think we'll see more minorities in SF now?

BUTLER: Well, let me put it this way: if it's okay to include human beings, I think it's okay to include minorities. As far as Williams is concerned, I don't really know. I was glad he was there, but watching Billy Dee Williams play that role was like watching *Jesus Christ Superstar* and realizing that we'd finally made it into biblical films: we could play Judas. Some book I read made the observation that they finally gave us a Black character in *Star Trek* and they made her a telephone operator.

I guess I don't like taking what I'm given. That's why I'm hoping there will be more Black SF writers, more Black writers period. Any minority group needs people who can speak from the group's perspective, maybe not speak from the group's perspective, maybe not speak for the whole group. But at least from a certain point of view and experience.

HARRISON: You speak of minorities and their place, or lack of place, in science fiction. What are your feelings about the view that a Black character should not be introduced unless his or her blackness is in some way significant to the story?

BUTLER: What it really means is that to be Black is to be abnormal. The norm is white, apparently, in the view of people who see things in that way. For them the only reason you would introduce a Black character is to introduce this kind of abnormality. Usually, it's because you're telling a story about racism or at least about race.

I've agreed to do an anthology with another writer. It's supposed to be an anthology about and by Black people. He sent me six stories that he thought would possibly be worth including. But . . . they were not stories about Black people. Except for one, they were all stories about racism. I wrote back to him about something I feel very strongly: racism is only one facet or aspect of Black existence. A lot of white writers (and some Black writers) see it as the totality of Black existence. What I want to do is pull in some good Black writers who will write about Black people and not just about how terrible it is to be hated.

HARRISON: How can science fiction's influence be used in a positive way in regard to minorities and women?

BUTLER: I see science fiction as a way of disseminating the fact that we don't have only one kind of people, namely white males, in this world. They are not the only ones who are here; not the only ones who count. It's very easy for a person who lives in a segregated neighborhood, either Black or white, who works at a job with only one kind of people, who goes to movies and watches TV (which is pretty white) to forget this fact. It's easy for a person, if it's a white person, to get the idea that they are really the only ones who matter. They may not think of it quite that way but that is the impression they internalize because of all that's around them. I think it is a writer's duty to write about human differences, all human differences, and help make them acceptable. I think SF writers can do this if they want to. In my opinion, they are a lot more likely to have a social conscience than other kinds of writers.

Science fiction writers like to think of themselves as progressive. They like to think of themselves as open-minded and it's possible in some cases to show them that they are lying to themselves when they portray the world as all-white or the universe as all-white.

HARRISON: There seems to be a widespread opinion that Blacks have had their day. Do you see the same happening to the women's movements?

BUTLER: Well, America is a country of fads. I don't think that it will happen to the women's movement. But it seems to me that the media is advertising the death of the women's movement. A vast majority of states have ratified the ERA but those few left are preventing the ERA from being added to the Constitution. I keep hearing, on TV talk shows (something I'm becoming addicted to), the attitude that somehow [the] ERA is not what people want. If it is what the people wanted, then it would have passed. These people often don't realize how many of the states have already ratified it. I don't mean to imply that there is some organized media campaign against the ERA, but since we're so faddish, and since the ERA is kind of old news, in a sense, it is being helped to die.

HARRISON: *Omni Magazine* recently quoted Dr. Savin, developer of the live virus oral vaccine for polio, as saying, "It may sound like a paradox, but my hope is that we may die, ultimately, in good health." When I read this, I thought of your character, Anyanwu, in *Wild Seed* who is able to look inside her body and detect which organ is malfunctioning and report or correct it. Does this lend some credence to the idea that SF is prophetic?

BUTLER: Science fiction can be prophetic although I hadn't really intended Anyanwu to be prophetic. I find myself in agreement with Savin, although I wonder how one would die of good health. Why wouldn't one just linger until senility or disintegration?

HARRISON: I was surprised to read an article, not too long ago, by a doctor who said it was really kind of silly to try to get rid of some of these diseases because, after all, we have to die from something. That might sound all right if you are hardened to watching people die, but I watched one person die of cancer and that was enough to start me thinking about characters like Anyanwu.

And yet, at one point in the novel, Anyanwu decided to shut herself off.

BUTLER: Yes. She had that much control over her body.

HARRISON: If we reach a point where people no longer die of physical diseases, what do you think will cause death?

BUTLER: Probably boredom. It is actually possible to die of boredom. Anyanwu had a different reason for dying. Actually, she and Doro (main characters in *Mind of My Mind* and *Wild Seed* with chameleonlike qualities) are different versions of what immortality could be. Doro is immortal and destructive. Anyanwu is immortal and creative. Her whole reason for deciding to die was being unable to tolerate Doro any longer although she was also unable to get along without him.

HARRISON: What changes have you seen in SF in the last ten years?

BUTLER: Science fiction is becoming a lot more human. We have a lot more women writers now. It really is remarkable how well the women characters have developed. Earlier SF tended to portray women as little dolls who were rewards for their heroes, or they were bitches . . . in other words, non-people. In a way, I suppose that this is similar to the stage Black people are going through; although I do find a lot more women who are interested in writing SF and who are doing it.

HARRISON: If indeed, science fiction is prophetic, do you, as a science fiction writer, have any prophecies to share? What kind of future do you see for humanity?

BUTLER: I am pessimistic about our real future. I see so many books about the future, both science fiction and popular science, telling us about the wonderful technological break-throughs that will make our lives so much better. But I never see anything about the sociological aspects of our future lives. Some science fiction people are thinking in terms of ecological problems, but the attitude in popular science seems to be, "Oh, we'll solve these problems; we always have."

For instance, there is the question of the nuclear waste from power plants. I'm not saying that it is going to destroy us all. It's just that I think it is a little dangerous to decide we will go ahead and make this stuff that is going to take more time than we have been civilized to deteriorate. But we assume that somehow, someday, someone will find a way to take care of it. I don't think people are paying enough attention to the long-term aspects of what we are doing to the earth. We are shortsighted. Especially in this country. I'm afraid that we are so used to having it good that what we want to do is find another way to have it just as good as we have always had it.

HARRISON: What do you see as the difference between the future as science fiction writers see it, and certain religious beliefs that say we are coming to our last days?

BUTLER: My mother is very religious so I'm very much aware of the attitude that these are the last days. But, let's face it, no matter where we have been in history, whoever has existed has been living in the last days . . . their own. When each of us dies the world ends for us. Not too long ago, I was at a science fiction convention, and we had a panel on religion. One of the topics was the fact that SF tends not to deal with religion, and when it does deal with it, it's with contempt. Science fiction seems more interested in machines than in people. It tends to dismiss religion. I don't think that's wise because religion has played such a large part in the lives of human beings throughout human history. In some ways, I wish we could outgrow it; I think at this point it does a lot of harm. But then, I'm fairly sure that if we do outgrow it, we'll find other reasons to kill and persecute each other. I wish we were able to depend on ethical systems that did not involve the Big Policeman in the sky. But I don't think this will happen. I'm not sure about the meaning of the born-again movement. It could be positive, but it could also be very destructive.

I see religion as something that really isn't controlling people and helping to channel their energy away from destruction. Sometimes it becomes destructive itself. It scares me. I was raised a born-again Baptist and I remember a minister from a different church coming to our church. He was really spewing out prejudice against the Jews and Catholics and anyone else who disagreed with him. Just as telling, he didn't get the kind of congregational feedback that you would expect from people who worshipped the Prince of Peace. The kind of religion that I'm seeing now is not the religion of love and it scares me. We need to outgrow it.

What we've done is create for ourselves the massive power of a Big Policeman in the sky. It would be nice if we would police ourselves. I think that in one way or another we will do ourselves in. Sooner or later the generation that says, "We're living our last days," really will be. But not because somebody strikes us from heaven. We'll do it to ourselves. And, to the future.

CALLALOO INTERVIEW

INTERVIEW BY RANDALL KENAN
CALLALOO
SPRING 1991

Octavia E. Butler is something of a phenomenon. Since 1976 she has published nine novels, more than any other Black woman in North America, and even more amazing, she writes science fiction. Having won all the major SF awards, (a Nebula and two Hugos), she has gained a substantial cult following, as well as critical acclaim, particularly for her 1979 novel, *Kindred*, reissued in 1988 in the prestigious Beacon Black Women Writers Series. *Kindred* is the tale of Dana Franklin, a Black woman from an interracial marriage in LA in 1976, who is mysteriously plucked back in time on a number of occasions to 1824 Maryland and to a moral dilemma involving her white ancestor. A book often compared to *Metamorphosis* for its uncannily successful blend of fact and fantasy, it is considered by many to be a modern classic. Butler manages to use the conventions of science fiction to subvert many long-held assumptions about race, gender and power; in her hands these devices become adept metaphors for reinterpreting and reconsidering our world. Strong women, multiracial societies and aliens who challenge humanity's penchant for destruction inform her work and lift it beyond genre. Her works include: *Patternmaster* (1976); *Mind of My Mind* (1977); *Survivor* (1978); *Wild Seed* (1980); *Clay's Ark* (1984);

and the Xenogenesis trilogy: *Dawn* (1987); *Adulthood Rites* (1988); and *Imago* (1989). Butler has also published a number of short stories and novellas, including the award-winning "Bloodchild" in 1984. She is working on the first book in a new series. Octavia Butler lives in Los Angeles. This phone interview took place on November 3, 1990.

RANDALL KENAN: Do you prefer to call your work speculative fiction, as opposed to science fiction or fantasy?

OCTAVIA BUTLER: No, actually I don't. Most of what I do is science fiction. Some of the things I do are fantasy. I don't like the labels, they're marketing tools, and I certainly don't worry about them when I'm writing. They are also inhibiting factors; you wind up not getting read by certain people, or not getting sold to certain people because they think they know what you write. You say science fiction and everybody thinks *Star Wars* or *Star Trek*.

KENAN: But the kind of constructs you use, like time travel for example in *Kindred*, or . . .

BUTLER: I mean literally, it is fantasy. There's no science in *Kindred*. I mean, if I was told that something was science fiction, I would expect to find something dealing with science in it. For instance, *Wild Seed* is more science fiction than most people realize. The main character is dealing with medical science, but she just doesn't know how to talk about it. With *Kindred* there's absolutely no science involved. Not even the time travel. I don't use a time machine or anything like that.

Time travel is just a device for getting the character back to confront where she came from.

KENAN: In earlier interviews you mentioned that there's an interesting parallel between your perception of your mother's life and some of the themes you explore in your work. You spoke of how in your growing up you saw her in an invisible role in her relationship with the larger society. How have certain ideas about your mother's life consciously or unconsciously affected your work?

BUTLER: My mother did domestic work and I was around sometimes when people talked about her as if she were not there, and I got to watch her going in back doors and generally being treated in a way that made me . . . I spent a lot of my childhood being ashamed of what she did, and I think one of the reasons I wrote *Kindred* was to resolve my feelings, because after all, I ate because of what she did . . . *Kindred* was a kind of reaction to some of the things going on during the sixties when people were feeling ashamed of, or more strongly, angry with their parents for not having improved things faster, and I wanted to take a person from today and send that person back to slavery. My mother was born in 1914 and spent her early childhood on a sugar plantation in Louisiana. From what she's told me of it, it wasn't that far removed from slavery, the only difference was they could leave, which eventually they did.

KENAN: I was also curious about the amount of research that you do when you're working on a book.

BUTLER: It varies greatly. With *Kindred*, I did go to Maryland and spend some time. Well, I mostly spent my time at the Enoch Pratt Free Library in Baltimore and at the Maryland Historical Society. I also went to the Eastern Shore to Talbot County, to Easton actually, and just walked around, wandered the streets and probably looked fairly disreputable. I didn't have any money at the time, so I did all my traveling by Greyhound and Trailways and I stayed at a horrible dirty little hotel . . . it was kind of frightening really . . . I didn't know what I was doing . . . I had missed the tours of the old houses for that year, I didn't realize that they were not ongoing but seasonal. Anyway, I went down to Washington, DC, and took a Gray Line bus tour of Mount Vernon and that was as close as I could get to a plantation. Back then they had not rebuilt the slave cabins and the tour guide did not refer to slaves but to "servants" and there was all this very carefully orchestrated dancing around the fact that it had been a slave plantation. But still I could get the layout, I could actually see things, you know, the tools used, the cabins that had been used for working. That, I guess, was the extent of my away-from-home research on *Kindred*. I did a lot more at the libraries.

KENAN: I'm assuming that entailed slave narratives and . . .

BUTLER: Yes, yes. Very much so. It was not fun . . . It's not pleasure reading. As a matter of fact, one of the things I realized when I was reading the slave narrative—I think I had gotten to one by a man who was explaining how he had been sold to a doctor who used him for medical experiments—was that I was not going to be able to come anywhere near presenting slavery as it was. I was going to have to do a somewhat cleaned-up version of slavery, or no one would be willing to read it. I think that's what most fiction writers do. They almost have to.

KENAN: But at the same time, I think you address the problem of accuracy and distance with amazing intelligence and depth. In place of visceral immediacy, you give us a new understanding of how far removed we are from manumission. For example, the scene where Dana in *Kindred* witnesses the patrollers catching the runaway, you address this issue straight on: how she was unprepared to bear witness to such horror. So at the same time, you are making the reader aware of how brutal it all is, was, and doubly, how much we're separated from that past reality and how television and movies have prejudiced us or in some cases blinded us to that fact.

BUTLER: The strange thing is with television and movies, I mean, they've made violence so cartoonishly acceptable . . . I was talking to a friend of mine the other day about the fact that some kids around the LA area, on Halloween, kids around fourteen and fifteen, found a younger child with Halloween candy and they shot him and took it away from him . . . Now when I was a kid, I knew bullies who beat up little kids and took away their candy, but it would not have occurred to them to go out with a knife or gun to do that, you know. This is a totally different subject, but it's one that interests me right now. Just what in the world is to be done, to bring back a sense of proportion of respect for life?

KENAN: But another thing that makes *Kindred* so painful and artful is the way that you translate the moral complexity and the choices that have to be made between Dana and her white husband and not only in the past but in the present.

BUTLER: I gave her that husband to complicate her life.

KENAN: And even though the roles in many ways are more affixed by society in the past, she has to make similar choices in the present; so it's almost as though time were an illusion.

BUTLER: Well, as I said, I was really dealing with some 1960s feelings when I wrote this book. So I'm not surprised that it strikes you that way; as a matter of fact I'm glad. I meant it to be complicated.

KENAN: Violence also seems to be a part of the fabric of your oeuvre, in a sense. The fact that Dana loses her arm, in *Kindred*, which is inexplicable on one level . . .

BUTLER: I couldn't really let her come all the way back. I couldn't let her return to what she was, I couldn't let her come back whole and that, I think, really symbolizes her not coming back whole. Antebellum slavery didn't leave people quite whole.

KENAN: But also, for instance, in "Bloodchild." [Note: In this story human beings on another planet have entered in a pact with an indigenous species who implant eggs in the humans for incubation. When the eggs hatch, the humans are cut open. Not everyone survives.] I mean, the idea that sacrifice has to be . . .

BUTLER: Not sacrifice. No, no . . .

KENAN: You wouldn't call it sacrifice? Cutting people open?

BUTLER: No, no . . . "Bloodchild" is very interesting in that men tend to see a horrible case of slavery, and women tend to see that, oh well, they had caesarians, big deal. [laughter]

KENAN: So really, you wouldn't characterize that as being violent?

BUTLER: Not anymore than . . . well, remember during the Middle Ages in Europe, I don't know what it was like in Africa, if a woman died giving birth, they would try to save the baby.

KENAN: Over the woman?

BUTLER: In this case, they were trying to save both of them and, I mean, it's not some horrible thing that I made up in that sense. In earlier science fiction there tended to be a lot of conquest: you land on another planet and you set up a colony and the natives have their quarters some place and they come in and work for you. There was a lot of that, and it was, you know, let's do Europe and Africa and South America all over again. And I thought no, no, if we do get to another world inhabited by intelligent beings, in the first place we're going to be at the end of a very, very, very long transport line. It isn't likely that people are going to be coming and going, you know, not even the way they did between England and this country, for instance. It would be a matter of a lifetime or more, the coming and going. So you couldn't depend on help from home. Even if you had help coming, it wouldn't help you. It might help your kids, if you survived to have any, but on the other hand it might not. So you are going to have to make some kind of deal with the locals: in effect, you're going to have to pay the rent. And that's pretty much what those people have done in "Bloodchild." They have made a deal. Yes, they can stay there but they are going to have to pay for it. And I don't see the slavery, and I don't see this as particularly barbaric. I mean, if human beings were able to make that good a deal with another species, I think it would be miraculous. [*laughs*] Actually, I think it would be immensely more difficult than that.

KENAN: Fascinating and faultlessly logical. But at the same time—again with the idea of violence—the relationship between Doro and Anyanwu in *Wild Seed*. That takes on a different paradigm. They are extremely violent to one another.

BUTLER: That's just men and women!

KENAN: But particularly in their various metamorphoses,

when she becomes a leopard, or the sheer number of people Doro kills. It's a sort of natural violence. Or a violence of survival, I should say . . .

BUTLER: It's not something I put there to titillate people, if that's what you mean. [*laughs*] I don't do that. As a matter of fact, I guess the worse violence is not between the two of them, but it's around them, it's what's happening to the people around them who are not nearly so powerful.

KENAN: In your work it does seem to be a given that this is a violent universe and you don't romanticize it in any respect.

BUTLER: I hope not; I haven't tried to. I think probably the most violent of my books were the early ones. A friend brought this to my attention the other day because she was just reading some of my stuff. She said that she was surprised at the amount of violence in *Patternmaster* and casual violence at that. [Note: The first in her Patternist novels, this book initiates the battle between the Patternists (humans with psionic powers) and the Clayarks (disease-mutated human quadrupeds).] I said it probably comes from how young I was when I wrote it. I think that it is a lot easier to not necessarily romanticize it, but to accept it without comment when you're younger. I think that men and women are more likely to be violent when they are younger.

KENAN: You have mentioned the African myths and lore that you used in *Wild Seed.* Can you talk more about that? I didn't realize that you had gone to such pains.

BUTLER: I used in particular, the myth of Atagbusi, who was an Onitsha Igbo woman. She was a shape-shifter who benefited her people while she was alive and when she died a market gate was named after her, a gate at the Onitsha market. It was believed that whoever used this market gate was under her protection . . . Doro comes from an adolescent fantasy of mine to live forever and breed people. And when I began to get a little more sense, I guess you could say, and started to work with Doro, I decided that he was going to be a Nubian, because I wanted him to be somehow associated with ancient Egypt. And by then his name was already Doro, and it would have been very difficult to change it. So I went to the library and got this poor, dog-eared, ragged Nubian-English dictionary. I looked up the word "Doro," and the word existed and it meant "the direction from which the sun comes," the east. That was perfect, especially since I had pretty much gotten Emma Daniels, who came before the name Anyanwu, but I had been looking through names for her, Igbo names, and I found a myth having to do with the sun and the moon. Anyway, the problem with that is, I lost it. I didn't write it down and I never found it again and all I had was one of the names: Anyanwu, meaning "the sun." That worked out perfectly with Doro, "the east." So I wound up putting them together.

KENAN: Such rich etymological and cultural resonance. It's almost as if the African lore itself is using you as a medium. Which leads me to a slightly different, but related topic. You seem to be exploring the idea of miscegenation on many different levels throughout your work. In Xenogenesis it seems to reach a new peak. [Note: In the trilogy, the alien Oankali join with human nuclear war survivors to create through genetic engineering a new species, better able to survive than both its progenitors.] Over the years you've been dealing with sex, race, gender; but here you're able to raise it yet another complicated step.

BUTLER: [*laughter*]

KENAN: Seriously. In *Kindred* miscegenation is quite literal. But in *Dawn*, *Adulthood Rites*, and *Imago*, genetics put an odd twist on an old idea.

BUTLER: One of the things that I was most embarrassed about in my novel *Survivor* is my human characters going off to another planet and finding other people they could immediately start having children with. Later I thought, oh well, you can't really erase embarrassing early work, but you don't have to repeat it. So I thought if I were going to bring people together from other worlds again, I was at least going to give them trouble. So I made sure they didn't have compatible sex organs, not to mention their other serious differences. And of course there are still a lot of biological problems that I ignore.

KENAN: How many other Black science fiction writers do you know personally?

BUTLER: I know two others personally. [Steve Barnes and Samuel R. Delany]

KENAN: Any other Black women?

BUTLER: I don't know any Black women who write science fiction. Lots of white women, but I don't know any Black women—which is not to say there aren't any. But I don't know any.

KENAN: I couldn't compare you to other winners of the Nebula and the Hugo Awards. When you interact with your fans, how do they react to your being Black and a woman? Is there a great deal of interest in the novelty of your being practically the only Black women sci-fi writer?

BUTLER: No. If they're curious about that, they tend not to tell me and I'm just as happy to have it that way. No, I've been in SF for a long time and I know people. I go to SF conventions and no matter where I go in the country, I generally see someone I know. SF is kind of a small town and there is no problem with enjoying yourself. Obviously, in some places you will meet with some nastiness, but it isn't general. The only place I was ever called "nigger," had someone scream "nigger" at me in public, was in Boston, for goodness sakes. It wasn't a person going to a conference, it was just a stranger who happened to see me standing, waiting for a traffic light with other SF people who were headed toward the convention.

KENAN: In light of that question, how do your readers react to the fact that most of your main protagonists are women and more often Black? Does that ever come up?

BUTLER: Yes, as a matter of fact it came up more before I was visible. I wrote three books before anybody knew who I was, aside from a few people here in LA. And I got a few letters asking why? The kind of letters that hedge around wondering why I write about Black people; but there were few such letters. People who are bigots probably don't want to talk to me. I hear signs of bigotry every now and then when someone slips up, someone's manners fail, or something slips out. But there isn't a lot of that kind of thing.

KENAN: Speaking of women in science fiction, a lot of Black women writers whom I've been in contact with lately speak of the ongoing debate between Black women and feminism. I'm sure the feminist debate is ongoing within science fiction. Do you find yourself at all caught up within that debate?

BUTLER: Actually it isn't very much. That flared up big during the seventies and now it's a foregone conclusion. Not that somebody is particularly a feminist, but if somebody is, it's their business . . . I was on a little early Sunday morning TV show a while back, and the hostess was a Black woman and there were two other Black women writers, a poet and a playwright and me. And the hostess asked as a near final question how we felt about feminism and the other two women said they didn't think much of it, they assumed it was for white people. I said that I thought it was just as important to have equal rights for women as it was to have equal rights for Black people and so I felt myself to be very much a feminist.

KENAN: And you feel your works then actively reflect feminist ideals?

BUTLER: Well, they do in a sense that women do pretty much what they want to do. One of the things that I wanted to deal with in the Xenogenesis books, especially the first one, was some of the old SF myths that kind of winked out during the seventies but were really prevalent before the seventies. Myths where, for instance, people crash-land on some other planet and all of a sudden they go back to "Me Tarzan, you Jane," and the women seem to accept this perfectly as all right, you know. We get given away like chattel and we get treated like . . . well, you get the picture. I thought I'd do something different.

KENAN: There seems to be a movement in your work from a view of continuance to a view of apocalypse. For instance, in *Clay's Ark* the civilization has been attacked by a microorganism. But in Xenogenesis there is a postapocalyptic scenario. Has your thinking about that changed? I understand there is a huge debate in science fiction now about writers who tend to wipe the population clean and start over again, as opposed to writers like William Gibson and the other cyberpunk writers, who take as a given that we are going to survive somehow, someway and then extrapolate from that assumption.

BUTLER: I don't think we are more likely to survive than any other species, especially considering that we have overspecialized ourselves into an interesting corner. But on the other hand, my new book isn't a postapocalyptic type of book. I'm not really talking about an earth that has been wiped clean of most people. As a matter of fact, Earth is as populated as ever and in fact more so because it takes place in the future. The greenhouse effect has intensified and there has been a certain amount of starvation and agricultural displacement. There are real problems. Some of our prime agricultural land won't be able to produce the crops that it's been producing and Canada will have the climate, but on the other hand Canada caught the brunt of the last few ice ages and has lost a lot of topsoil, which wound up down here. These are big problems and they are not sexy as problems, so they are not the prime problems in the series that I am working on, but they're in the background. It's not a postapocalyptic book, it's a book in which society has undergone severe changes, but continues.

KENAN: I am really impressed by the way your characters often speak, almost epigrammatically, not to say that it is stiff dialogue, but you achieve a sort of majesty, particularly when you're talking about the human species, how we interact with one another. There is a lot of wisdom in what you have your characters say, without sounding didactic. What are your literary influences to that effect, both science fiction and nonscience fiction, what writers?

BUTLER: All sorts of things influence me. I let things influence me. If they catch my interest, I let them take hold. When I was growing up I read mostly science fiction. I remember getting into Harlan Ellison's class and at one point having him say, science fiction fans read too much science fiction; and he was no doubt right, but as an adolescent that was all I read except for schoolwork. I guess the people that I learned the most from were not necessarily the best writers (although Theodore Sturgeon was one of them and I think he was definitely one of the best writers). They were people who impressed me with their ideas. I didn't know what good writing was frankly, and I didn't have any particular talent for writing so I copied a lot of the old pulp writers in the way I told a story. Gradually I learned that that wasn't the way I wanted to write. But as for what influences me now, well, for instance I was reading a book about Antarctica . . . It was a kind of a difficult book to read because it involved so much suffering. Antarctica is probably as close to another planet as we've got on this earth . . . I thought what if I had a bunch of outcasts who had to go live in a very uncertain area and I made it a parched, devastated part of future Southern California because there are areas here where the hills fall into the canyons and cliffs crumble off into the sea even without earthquakes to help them along. My characters go to this ruined place as though it were another world and the people they meet there are adapted to their new environment. They won't be savages crawling through the hills. I wanted them to have found some other way to cope because obviously some people would have to. Not everybody would go ape or become members of gangs and go around killing people. There would be some people who would try to put together a decent life, whatever their problems were . . . Really, I think that's what I mean about something influencing me. The book I read didn't influence me to write about Antarctica, but it influenced me to take a piece of the earth as we know it and see what it could become without playing a lot of special effects games.

KENAN: Are there other literary or nonliterary sources that you see consciously or unconsciously affected your work?

BUTLER: Every place I've lived is a nonliterary influence, every place and every person who has impressed me enough to keep my attention for a while. If something attracts my attention I am perfectly willing to follow that interest. I can remember when I was writing *Clay's Ark*, I would be listening to the news and I would hear something and it would be immediately woven into the novel. As a matter of fact some of the things that I found out after I finished *Clay's Ark* were even more interesting. Down in El Salvador, I guess about a year after I finished *Clay's Ark*, I read that it was the habit of many of the rich people to armor-plate Jeep Wagoneers and use them as family cars and that's exactly the vehicle that my character was using and I was glad I had chosen well.

KENAN: Science fiction writers—with a few notable exceptions like Samuel Delany—are often slapped about the wrists because people feel that their writing styles are wooden and are merely there to get the plot across. Your writing has almost biblical overtones at times. Have you consciously striven for such a style?

BUTLER: I've developed my love for words late in life really. I guess it was when I realized that I was writing pulp early on. I realized I didn't want to. I read some of my own writing, which is a very painful thing to do, and I could see what was the matter with it, having gotten some distance in time from it. And I realized that there were things that I would have to learn even before that. Back during the 1960 election and the Kennedy Administration, that was when I began to develop into a news junkie. I was very interested in Kennedy and I would listen to his speeches and I guess I was about thirteen when he was elected, and I realized that half the time I couldn't figure out what he was saying and I felt really, really bad about that. I felt stupid. Although I didn't know it at the time, I'm a bit dyslexic. I realized that there was so much more to learn. You're always realizing there is so much out there that you don't know. That's when I began to teach myself as opposed to just showing up at school. I think that there comes a time when you just have to do that, when things have to start to come together for you or you don't really become an educated person. I suspect that has been the case for a lot of people, they just never start to put it all together.

KENAN: Obviously, you write beautifully. So is it all organic in the sense that all these disparate ideas and themes fit together, that your interests coincided?

BUTLER: No, it's work. But you mean style. Yes, and it's something I can't talk about. It's very, very intimate. I make signs. The wall next to my desk is covered in signs and maps. The signs are to remind myself sometimes of things. For instance, a sign from a book called *The Art of Dramatic Writing* by Lajos Egri, it's a kind of a paraphrasing really; tension and conflict can be achieved through uncompromising characters in a death struggle. And just having signs on my wall to remind me of certain things that I need to remember to do in the writing—signs in black indelible ink. That sort of thing, it's kind of juvenile but it really helps me. But there are some things about the writing that are just so personal that you can't even talk about them.

KENAN: I should ask in closing: Do you have any advice for young writers?

BUTLER: I have advice in just a few words. The first, of course, is to read. It's surprising how many people think they want to be writers but they don't really like to read books.

KENAN: *Amen!*

BUTLER: And the second is to write, every day, whether you like it or not. Screw inspiration. The third is to forget about talent, whether or not you have any. Because it doesn't really matter. I mean, I have a relative who is extremely gifted musically, but chooses not to play music for a living. It is her pleasure, but it is not her living. And it could have been. She's gifted; she's been doing it ever since she was a small child and everyone has always been impressed with her. On the other hand, I don't feel that I have any particular literary talent at all. It was what I wanted to do, and I followed what I wanted to do, as opposed to getting a job doing something that would make more money, but it would make me miserable. This is the advice that I generally give to people who are thinking about becoming writers.

KENAN: I don't know if I would agree that you have no literary talent. But that's your personal feeling.

BUTLER: It's certainly not a matter of sitting there and having things fall from the sky.

"THERE ISN'T ANYTHING I CAN'T DO IN SCIENCE FICTION"

INTERVIEW BY TERRY GROSS
FRESH AIR
DECEMBER 14, 1993

TERRY GROSS: This is *Fresh Air*. I'm Terry Gross. My guest has won science fiction's two highest honors, the Nebula Award and the Hugo Award. Octavia Butler is one of the few African American women in the genre. She's described herself as a pessimist if I'm not careful, a feminist always, a Black, a quiet egoist, and a former Baptist. She's more interested in social criticism than high-tech hardware. She uses the genre to write about racial conflict and sexual identity. Butler's novel *Kindred* was about the legacy of slavery. The main character has transported back to a pre-Civil War plantation. Butler's Xenogenesis series is about alien beings who are undifferentiated by gender. Her new novel, *Parable of the Sower*, is set in Southern California in the year 2025. The people lucky enough to still have houses have to build walls to protect themselves against crazy and desperate street people . . .

OCTAVIA E. BUTLER: It's grim. All the things that I can see going wrong now, well, not all of them, but a good many of them have continued to go wrong. In 2025, for instance, the things that work best are the tax system. I mean, everybody still has to pay their taxes. A lot of people don't have jobs and are living on the street. Even though they work very hard, they're not able to earn enough to both live in a house and eat food. That sounds familiar, but in this case, it's more like India. It's Los Angeles. It's more like India with whole families living camped out on the street, and it's so ordinary, so unremarkable, that nobody pays any attention. It's not unusual to see horribly wounded people on the street because of whatever happened the night before. It's just a society that's on the base, just about ready to collapse.

TERRY GROSS: There's a lot of arsonists in the society that you've created.

BUTLER: One of the things I've done is create a drug that makes people watch fire and get a sexual high from it. And naturally, this causes a lot of arson.

GROSS: There's a paragraph about arson that I'd like you to read from your novel.

BUTLER: Okay. [*reading*] It's Christmas Eve. Last night, someone set fire to the Payne-Parrish house. While the community tried to put out the fire and then tried to keep it from spreading, three other houses were robbed. Ours was one of the three. Thieves broke in, took all our store-bought food, wheat flour, sugar, canned goods, packaged goods. They took our radio, too, our last one. The crazy thing is, before we went to bed, we had been listening to a half-hour news feature about increasing arson. People are setting more fires to cover crimes, although why they bother these days, I don't know. The police are no threat to criminals. People are setting fires to do what our arsonists did last night, to get the neighbors of the arson victim to leave their homes unguarded. People are setting fires to get rid of whomever they dislike, from personal enemies to anyone who looks or sounds foreign or racially different. People are setting fires because they're frustrated, angry, hopeless. They have no power to improve their lives, but they have the power to make others even more miserable. And the only way to prove to yourself that you have power is to use it.

GROSS: People create fires in your novel, in part to get people out of their homes so that the arsonists can steal everything from the home while the people have run out. How did you—

BUTLER: The neighboring homes, in particular.

GROSS: In the neighboring homes, right. Yeah, so how did you get this idea of arson?

BUTLER: Well, I suspect you're asking if it came from the riots. Is that what you were thinking about?

GROSS: I wasn't, but that's not a bad question.

BUTLER: Yeah, because I've been asked that several times, and the truth is I've been working on this novel for about four years. I worked at it for three years trying to write it, and finally during 1992, I did write it and was just about done with the basic draft of it when the riots came along. So the idea didn't come out of that, but people have set fires for odd reasons, have done a great deal of harm for odd reasons. And one of the things I have noticed about people is that if they have a little bit of power, the only way they can, as I said in the book, prove they have it, is to use it.

GROSS: The main character in your novel has what you've called hyper-empathy. In other words, she experiences other people's pain—

BUTLER: As though it were her own.

GROSS: —as though it were her own. So in this very violent society, every time she's in proximity to somebody who has a gunshot wound or a stabbing wound, she feels that pain as if she had been shot or stabbed.

BUTLER: I wanted to make sure that I wrote a novel in which everything that happened actually could happen. None of this is parapsychological. There's no telepathy or anything involved. It's delusional. I mean, it doesn't help her that it's delusional, that she only thinks she feel these things, but it is delusional on her part. It's a result of her mother having taken a drug.

GROSS: I think part of what you're trying to say with this hyper-empathy is that if people really felt other people's pain, we couldn't possibly live in a violent society. It would hurt too much.

BUTLER: I thought so. When I began writing the book, I

honestly thought that was what I was going to wind up doing. I thought hyper-empathy was something that I would find some way to spread to other people, but somewhere in the book I realized . . . In writing the book, I realized that no, people would find ways. They would find ways to carry on violence. For one thing, the hyper-empaths are very vulnerable. They are, as my character's brother says, almost natural slaves. It's much easier to abuse them than to abuse other people.

GROSS: Did that come at all from the knowledge that a writer has to be very empathic, or is the word "empathetic"?

BUTLER: I'm not sure which word. I know what you mean.

GROSS: Because you have to really feel everything your characters are feeling, and you probably have to imagine the feelings of the people around you to imagine what they're feeling so that you could write about it at some future point.

BUTLER: One of the things that I can remember in my growing up, writers mine their own lives. You've probably run across this with others and—

GROSS: I try to mine their lives, too.

BUTLER: Right. In my life, especially when I was very young, I can remember getting very upset about things that happened that seemed to be hurting people and things that weren't upsetting anyone else. I can remember after a while,

I used to watch a lot of television as a kid, and for a long time I watched, oh, cowboy shows or whatever, where people got beaten up or hit with chairs or guns or whatever. And at first it meant nothing to me, and then we were in a car accident and I got a hard crack on the head, and thereafter, I really empathized with anyone who was hit on the head, and I got so that I really didn't want to watch that for a while. I still don't like to watch it, but for a while there, I stopped watching that sort of television.

GROSS: It literally hurt you to see it, so this connects to the hyper-empathy.

BUTLER: I think probably most kids empathize too much at some point in their lives and have to grow out of it, are forced to grow out of it, just to survive, and my character is a person who can't grow out of it and for whom it is literal. She doesn't just empathize in the sense of psychologically sharing, but she really seems to feel it physically.

GROSS: You're one of the few African Americans and one of the fewer African American women writing in the genre of science fiction. What speaks to you about the genre?

BUTLER: I write science fiction because, first of all, I like it. I always liked it. When I was a kid, I read it and enjoyed it and it was one of the first things that I began writing. I also write it because it offers me such freedom. There isn't anything that I can't do in science fiction, past, present, future, Black, white,

Hispanic, Asian, whatever. I can get away with all sorts of things in science fiction and fantasy, I should say, that might not be that possible in trade fiction.

GROSS: How have you addressed issues of race and gender in your books?

BUTLER: Well, for instance, I did a book called *Kindred,* in which a Black character goes back in time to the antebellum South, not voluntarily, of course, and experiences slavery firsthand. *Kindred* is apparently still popular, still being used as a textbook in high school and college.

GROSS: As a woman and as an African American, are there things that bothered you about the science fiction books that you read when you were first starting to read them?

BUTLER: Yes. I wasn't in them.

GROSS: Yeah, right. And I don't know if this is just true of a certain type of science fiction movie and TV show, but it always seemed that when a type of male writer looked into the future, what he saw was women wearing a lot less with a lot more cleavage.

BUTLER: Right. Yeah. I read a lot of science fiction as a kid, and of course, that meant reading boys' books because that's what kids' science fiction was. I made up my own stories to put myself in them. I wound up writing science fiction from the point of view of girls and women, just because I was a girl and I am a woman. I wound up writing science fiction from the point of view of Black people because I am Black, but I've also explored, and in a strange sense, I suppose, found out what it might be like to be a white male or an Oriental or whatever. One of the things writing does is allow you to be other people without actually being locked up for it.

GROSS: We're talking empathy here, right?

BUTLER: Yes.

GROSS: When you entered the science fiction genre, were there a lot of women, were there a lot of African Americans reading science fiction, and did your publisher worry about your books finding a natural market?

BUTLER: When I got into science fiction, I sold my first three books without an agent and with no particular connections. I just mailed them in over the transom so nobody knew who I was and nobody knew I was Black and no, apparently there wasn't any worrying. I didn't have any difficulty selling my first three novels. When I wrote *Kindred*, which is unmistakably of special interest to Black people, I had a lot of trouble. All of a sudden, fifteen publishers couldn't find a place for it. They didn't know how to sell it, and I have letters saying, "Oh, we really like it. It's wonderful. We just don't know what to do with it. Maybe you could make it a romance or maybe you could make it a juvenile." They just had no idea how to sell it as what it was.

GROSS: So how was it finally sold?

BUTLER: It was sold as a trade book, mainstream fiction, and pretty much ignored for a while, I guess. And then when Beacon Press brought it back, it all of a sudden began to get a lot of the attention that I'd hoped it would get originally.

GROSS: If you're just joining us, my guest is Octavia Butler and she's won both the Nebula and the Hugo Awards. Those are the highest prizes in America for science fiction. Her new novel is called *Parable of the Sower*. We're going to take a short break and then we'll talk some more. This is *Fresh Air*.

Back with science fiction writer Octavia Butler. Now, your new novel, *Parable of the Sower*, opens with the main character getting baptized in the name of the God that isn't hers anymore. Her father is a preacher, but she stopped believing in his God three years before. Now, were you raised in a religious family?

BUTLER: Baptist, yes. My father died when I was a baby, so I didn't have the very religious father to live up to, but I had the experience myself of getting baptized when I no longer believed, just because I didn't have the courage to say so to my mother.

GROSS: How did that feel to get baptized, knowing that you didn't believe?

BUTLER: Very bad. In a way I felt cowardly because I had absorbed the idea that you shouldn't tell lies and you should especially not lie about things that important, but on the other hand, I had rejected the religion, so it was a strange feeling for me. I didn't feel that something rotten or terrible was going to happen to me or anything like that. I just felt that I was being really seriously dishonest.

GROSS: Did you feel that that dishonesty would hurt your family less than the honesty would?

BUTLER: No, I was just being cowardly.

GROSS: How old were you?

BUTLER: Thirteen, twelve, thirteen.

GROSS: When did you actually leave the church?

BUTLER: When I was seventeen or eighteen. I was a big-mouthed kid. I announced to my mother that I no longer believed, and she had a fit and worried that I was going to be lost and go to hell and the usual. I guess, really, in your teens is the best time to do a thing like that. One of the reasons I made my character a teenager when she begins all this is because only a teenager would be dumb enough to try to start such a thing, and only a teenager would have any chance of succeeding, just because she doesn't know how impossible the situation is.

GROSS: Now, you grew up on a chicken farm in California?

BUTLER: Well, I lived there for about a year. Actually, I grew up in Pasadena, California.

GROSS: Oh, I see.

BUTLER: Yeah. My grandmother had a chicken ranch. My father died when I was very young, and my mother, trying to get her life together, left me with my grandmother for a while, so I did have a chance to live on the chicken ranch for a little while.

GROSS: What did your father die of?

BUTLER: Oh, overdoing just about everything.

GROSS: What happened?

BUTLER: Oh, huge man, ate too much, drank too much, died young.

GROSS: Was the farm a farm your grandmother owned?

BUTLER: Yes, yes. My grandmother was an amazing woman. She was an orphan and she made her own way. She married very young. I think she was actually about twelve when she married, and she married a much older man and had several children, and he died and left her, naturally, he was considerably older and she had to make a way for her children. She was in Southern Louisiana originally. She was doing things like cutting sugarcane and cleaning houses, and she left her children with relatives, went to California, found work cleaning houses and doing anything else that she could find, sent for her children, and kept working incredibly hard and began to buy property. And that's how she eventually wound up with the ranch and a house and a truck for hauling and several other things that should have been out of her reach, I think would've been if she had been a lesser woman.

GROSS: Was that inspirational to you?

BUTLER: Very much so. She was a very strong woman. As a matter of fact, I used her as a pattern for the main character of a book called *Wild Seed*.

GROSS: What kind of work did your mother do?

BUTLER: My mother was taken out of school at age ten. My mother was the oldest girl. And custom of the time, I guess the oldest boy was allowed to go on going to school and the oldest girl was taken out of school and put to work, so she only had a few years' education, and she did housework most of her life and eventually nurse's aide work.

GROSS: You once said that you needed your fantasies when you were young to shield you from the world. What was especially bad about the world when you were growing up?

BUTLER: I think because my mother and her brothers and

sisters grew up during the Depression and actually did know times when there was no food and when they were just about on the street, they had the idea that life, well, I suppose it's not that unusual an idea, that not only was life hard, but any job you could get, any work you could do, you should stick with it no matter how unpleasant it was. You should put up with any amount of tiresome behavior on the part of your employer. Life is hell and you have to put up with it, and then after you've put up with it for a while, you get to go to heaven. This didn't seem like anything I really wanted to grow up to.

GROSS: That's sometimes a hard pattern to change.

BUTLER: I was an only child and I guess you could say very much my own person. I constructed my own world as I went along. I accepted the idea that you had to work for a living, but I didn't accept the idea that you had to do something you hated just because it paid.

GROSS: Writing must have seemed like a real long shot because—

BUTLER: Oh, gosh, yeah. Everybody in the family said, "Oh, you can write in your spare time and you can write as a hobby, whatever," but the idea of writing for a living was completely alien.

GROSS: When you were young and started writing stories, were the adults ever worried about you because of the kinds of stories you were caught up in? Did they seem unhealthy for a child?

BUTLER: My mother at one point took in elderly roomers, and I can remember telling them stories, and one of them in particular, my favorite old woman, she used to be a carnival mentalist and I adopted—

GROSS: Oh, wow.

BUTLER: Yeah. I adopted her as a step-grandmother, even though we were not related at all. My mother took in older people who weren't quite ready for the nursing home but who didn't want to live alone any longer, and had them paying as roomers. She told my mother that maybe I was going a little far and maybe . . . She seemed to think that I didn't know that I was telling stories, that they were fiction, and that maybe I actually believed them and maybe I needed a little help, so she was the main one who thought that maybe it was unhealthy for me to be doing that.

GROSS: Well, tell me more about this carnival mentalist. Did she use a lot of trickery?

BUTLER: She was a wonderful old lady. She used to scare the heck out of me. No, I never knew her to use any trickery at all. She knew people. She'd been alive for a long time. She was an observer of humanity and she knew how to hold your attention and she knew how to take you in.

GROSS: How would she take you in? Do you remember any of the—

BUTLER: Well, it wasn't a matter of what she said. It was more her manner, that you accepted her word for things and if she told you something frightening, you worried about it. You definitely worried about it.

GROSS: Did she give you things to worry about?

BUTLER: Only if I annoyed her, which I tended to do because I liked her and I would hang around and talk too much.

GROSS: Now, she was the one who thought that you were maybe too taken up with the stories, right? Did that scare you? Did you think maybe you were?

BUTLER: No. No, not at all. I didn't have confidence in myself in social situations, but I was confident within myself, that I knew what was real, which is probably an arrogant thing for anybody to feel, but I did feel that I knew what was real and I wasn't having any problems with my fantasies.

GROSS: Getting back to empathy again, your character with hyper-empathy, this becomes a bad thing for her because she feels other people's pain too much, and it's a delusion that makes it impossible for her to be around people who are suffering without suffering herself. We always think of empathy as a very good thing. Why did you make empathy into a bad thing?

BUTLER: Because it can be a weakness. I mentioned being too empathetic, if that's the word, as a child. It can make you cringe when you should be offering help, and in her case, even more so because she's actually feeling physical pain, or as good as. It's a weakness if it cripples you and it cripples her.

GROSS: Octavia Butler's new novel is called *Parable of the Sower.*

"WE KEEP PLAYING THE SAME RECORD"

INTERVIEW BY STEPHEN W. POTTS
SCIENCE FICTION STUDIES
FEBRUARY 1996

For readers of this journal, Octavia E. Butler literally needs no introduction. Her exquisite, insightful works—especially the three Xenogenesis novels (*Dawn*, *Adulthood Rites*, *Imago*) and her award-winning story "Bloodchild"—have been discussed and analyzed more than once in these pages.

One usually has to get up early in the morning to reach Ms. Butler. A private person, she prefers writing in the predawn hours and by 8:00 a.m. is frequently out of the house on the day's business. She has other claims to uniqueness: she is a native of Los Angeles who does not drive; she is a woman of color working in a genre that has almost none; and she is a science fiction author who has received a prestigious literary award, to wit, a 1995 grant from the MacArthur Foundation.

The following conversation took place by telephone early one morning in February 1996. It has been edited only to eliminate digressions, redundancies, and irrelevancies and to bridge some technical difficulties; Ms. Butler was given the opportunity to review and amend the finished version.

STEPHEN W. POTTS: Your name has been turning up with increasing frequency in journals (such as *Science Fiction Studies*) devoted to the serious study of science fiction. Do you read reviews or literary criticism of your work?

OCTAVIA E. BUTLER: I do, but I tend to get angry. Not when I disagree with someone's interpretation, but when people clearly have not read the whole book. I'm not too upset when they are factually wrong about some incident, which can happen to anybody, but I am when they are inaccurate about something sweeping. For example, somebody writing a review of *Parable of the Sower* said, "Oh, the Earthseed religion is just warmed-over Christianity," and I thought this person could not have been troubled to read the Earthseed verses and just drew that conclusion from the title.

POTTS: I ask because a substantial part of modern literary theory dwells on relationships of power and on the human body as a site of conflict: between men and women, among classes and races, between imperial and colonial peoples. These issues intersect nicely with the subject matter of your fiction. I was wondering if you were at all familiar with cultural theory.

BUTLER: Ah. No, I avoid all critical theory because I worry about it feeding into my work. I mean, I don't worry about nonfiction in general feeding in—in fact, I hope it will—but I worry about criticism influencing me because it can create a vicious circle or something worse. It's just an impression of mine, but in some cases critics and authors seem to be massaging each other. It's not very good for storytelling.

POTTS: The first work of yours I read was the story "Bloodchild" in its original printing in *Asimov's*. I remember being particularly impressed that you had taken the invading bug-eyed monster of classic science fiction and turned it into a seductively nurturing, maternal figure.

BUTLER: It is basically a love story. There are many different kinds of love in it: family love, physical love . . . The alien needs the boy for procreation, and she makes it easier on him by showing him affection and earning his in return. After all, she is going to have her children with him.

POTTS: In fact, she will impregnate him.

BUTLER: Right. But so many critics have read this as a story about slavery, probably just because I am Black.

POTTS: I was going to ask you later about the extent to which your work addresses slavery.

BUTLER: The only places I am writing about slavery is where I actually say so.

POTTS: As in *Kindred*.

BUTLER: And in *Mind of My Mind* and *Wild Seed*. What I was trying to do in "Bloodchild" was something different with the invasion story. So often you read novels about humans colonizing other planets and you see the story taking one of two courses. Either the aliens resist and we have to conquer them violently, or they submit and become good servants. In the latter case, I am thinking of a specific novel, but I don't want to mention it by name. I don't like either of those alternatives, and I wanted to create a new one. I mean, science fiction is supposed to be about exploring new ideas and possibilities. In the case of "Bloodchild," I was creating an alien that was different from us, though still recognizable—a centipede-like creature. But you're not supposed to regard it as evil.

POTTS: Something similar is going on in the Xenogenesis trilogy, isn't it? While teaching the books in my university classes, I have encountered disagreement over which species comes off worse, the humans or the Oankali. Humanity has this hierarchical flaw, particularly in the male, but the Oankali are the ultimate users, adapting not only the entire human genome for its own purposes but ultimately destroying the planet for all other life as well. Are we supposed to see a balance of vices here?

BUTLER: Both species have their strengths and weaknesses. You have small groups of violent humans, but we don't see all humans rampaging as a result of their contradiction. For the most part, the Oankali do not force or rush humans into mating but try to bring them in gradually. In fact, in *Adulthood Rites*, the construct Akin convinces the Oankali that they cannot destroy the human beings who refuse to participate. The Oankali decide that humans do deserve an untouched world of their own, even if it's Mars.

POTTS: In the case of both humans and Oankali, you offer sociobiological arguments for behavior: humans are bent toward destroying themselves and others; the Oankali are biologically driven to co-opt the genome of other species and to literally rip off their biospheres. Do you largely accept sociobiological principles?

BUTLER: Some readers see me as totally sociobiological, but that is not true. I do think we need to accept that our behavior *is* controlled to some extent by biological forces. Sometimes a small change in the brain, for instance—just a few cells—can completely alter the way a person or animal behaves.

POTTS: Are you thinking of Oliver Sacks's books, such as *The Man Who Mistook His Wife for a Hat*?

BUTLER: Exactly. Or the fungus that causes tropical ants to climb trees to spread its spores, or the disease that makes a wildebeest spend its last days spinning in circles. But I don't accept what I would call classical sociobiology. Sometimes we can work around our programming if we understand it.

POTTS: The exploitation of reproduction and, by extension, of family arises in a number of your works. Doro in the Patternist novels is breeding a master race and uses family ties with heroines like Anyanwu in *Wild Seed* and Mary in *Mind of My Mind* to help keep them under control. Family ties control the problematic bond between Dana and Rufus in *Kindred*. Reproduction and family lie at the crux of the relationship in "Bloodchild" and between the humans and Oankali in Xenogenesis. Do you intentionally focus on reproductive and family issues as a central theme, or did this just happen?

BUTLER: Perhaps as a woman, I can't help dwelling on the importance of family and reproduction. I don't know how men feel about it. Even though I don't have a husband and children, I have other family, and it seems to me our most important set of relationships. It is so much of what we are. Family does not have to mean purely biological relationships either. I know families that have adopted outside individuals; I don't mean legally adopted children but other adults, friends, people who simply came into the household and stayed. Family bonds can even survive really terrible abuse.

POTTS: Of course, you show the power of such bonds operating in either direction; for instance, Anyanwu in *Wild Seed* and Dana in *Kindred* both ultimately take advantage of the fact that their respective "masters" need them.

BUTLER: They don't recognize these men as their masters.

POTTS: I was putting the word in quotation marks. Are you suggesting that people in subordinate positions should recognize and exploit what power they do have?

BUTLER: You do what you have to do. You make the best use of whatever power you have.

POTTS: We even see that humans have more power than they realize over the Oankali. Especially with the construct Ooloi in *Imago*: they have no identity without human mates. Aaor devolves into a slug.

BUTLER: The constructs are an experiment. They do not know what they are going to be, or when it is going to happen. And they do not need humans specifically, even though they prefer them; they can bond with anything. But they have to bond.

POTTS: I would like to go back a bit in your literary history. Who were your authorial influences as an apprentice writer?

BUTLER: I read a lot of science fiction with absolutely no discrimination when I was growing up—I mean, good, bad, or awful [*laughs*]. It didn't matter. I remember latching onto people and reading everything I could find by them, people like John Brunner, who wrote a lot. I could pick up Ace Doubles at the used-book store for a nickel or a dime, so I was always reading John Brunner. And Theodore Sturgeon— by the time I was reading adult science fiction, he had a considerable body of work. Of course, Robert A. Heinlein. I can remember my very first adult science fiction, a story called "Lorelei of the Red Mist." If I am not mistaken, it was Ray Bradbury's first published story. Leigh Brackett began it and he finished it.

POTTS: Can you think of anybody outside of science fiction?

BUTLER: I tended to read whatever was in the house, which meant that I read a lot of odd stuff. Who was that guy that used to write about men's clubs all the time? John O'Hara. It was Mars for me. I like British between-the-wars mysteries for the same reason. They take place on Mars; they're different worlds.

POTTS: Might we suggest that since John O'Hara writes about upper-class white culture, his world would be almost as alien to you as the worlds of science fiction?

BUTLER: Absolutely. There was a book of his stories in the house, as well as books by James Thurber and James Baldwin. I did not read any Langston Hughes until I was an adult, but I remember being carried away by him and Gwendolyn Brooks. When I was growing up, the only Blacks you came across in school were slaves—who were always well treated—and later, when we got to individuals, Booker T. Washington and George Washington Carver. Booker T. Washington started a college, and Carver did something with peanuts; we never knew what. We did not read anything by a Black writer except [James Weldon] Johnson's "The Creation," and that was in high school. We managed to get through adolescence without being introduced to any Black culture.

POTTS: I was in that same generation, and I remember that it wasn't really until the seventies that we started opening up the canon. Actually, the issue is still controversial, judging from the so-called culture war over how inclusive the canon should be or whether we should even have one.

BUTLER: Yes, it's too bad when . . . well, there was one person I had a lot of respect for, but he could not find a single Black person to put into the canon, so I lost my respect for him rather badly.

POTTS: On its surface, *Parable of the Sower* looks like a change in direction from your earlier work.

BUTLER: Not really. It is still fundamentally about social power.

POTTS: But it is much more a close extrapolation from current trends: the increasing class gap, the fear of crime, the chaos of the cities spreading to the suburbs, the centrifugal forces tearing our society apart.

BUTLER: Yes. It really distresses me that we see these things happening now in American society when they don't have to. Some people insist that all civilizations have to rise and fall—like the British before us—but we have brought this on ourselves. What you see today has happened before: a few powerful people take over with the approval of a class below them who has nothing to gain and even much to lose as a result. It's like the Civil War: most of the men who fought to preserve slavery were actually being hurt by it. As farmers they could not compete with the plantations, and they could not even hire themselves out as labor in competition with the slaves who could be hired out more cheaply by their owners. But they supported the slave system anyway.

POTTS: They probably opposed affirmative action.

BUTLER: [*laughs*] Right. I guess many people just need someone to feel superior to to make themselves feel better. You see Americans doing it now, unfortunately, while voting against their own interests. It is that kind of shortsighted behavior that is destroying us.

POTTS: Are these problems somehow unique to American society?

BUTLER: Oh no, of course not.

POTTS: I was sure you'd say that.

BUTLER: We are seeing a particular American form here, but look at the Soviet Union. When capitalism took over, it is amazing how quickly they developed a crime problem. Unfortunately, the most successful capitalists over there now seem to be the criminals.

POTTS: Which is ironic because in classic Soviet Marxist theory the capitalist class was associated with the criminal class.

BUTLER: That may be the problem. We are getting into murky territory here: I heard about an old man in Russia who tried to turn his farm into a successful private enterprise, but his neighbors came over and destroyed his efforts. He was not a criminal, but to them that kind of individualistic profit making was criminal behavior. I guess to succeed in

Russia you have to be someone who (a) doesn't care what the neighbors think and (b) has a bodyguard. And if you're in that position, you probably are a criminal.

POTTS: To get back to *Parable of the Sower*, Lauren Olamina is empathic—

BUTLER: She is not empathic. She feels herself to be. Usually in science fiction "empathic" means that you really are suffering, that you are actively interacting telepathically with another person, and she is not. She has this delusion that she cannot shake. It's kind of biologically programmed into her.

POTTS: Interesting. So what is happening, say, when she feels the pain of the wounded dog she ends up killing?

BUTLER: Oh, even if it is not there, she feels it. In the first chapter of the book, she talks about her brother playing tricks on her—pretending to be hurt, pretending to bleed, and causing her to suffer. I have been really annoyed with people who claim Lauren is a telepath, who insist that she has this power. What she has is a rather crippling delusion.

POTTS: So we should maintain some ironic distance from her?

BUTLER: No.

POTTS: We should still identify with her.

BUTLER: I hope readers will identify with all my characters, at least while they're reading.

POTTS: Through Earthseed, Lauren hopes to bring back a sense of communal purpose and meaning by turning people's eyes back to the stars. It made me think: the space program of the sixties really was part of the general hopefulness of the decade, part of our sense that anything was possible if we strove together as a people.

BUTLER: And that was the decade of my adolescence. We keep playing the same record. Earlier I was talking about it: we begin something and then we grow it to a certain point and then it destroys itself or else it is destroyed from the outside—whether it is Egypt or Rome or Greece, this country or Great Britain, you name it. I do feel that we are either going to continue to play the same record until it shatters—and I said it in the book, though not in those words—or we are going to do something else. And I think the best way to do something else is to go someplace else where the demands on us will be different. Not because we are going to go someplace else and change ourselves, but because we will go someplace else and be forced to change.

POTTS: Do you think we will be better for that change?

BUTLER: It's possible. We could be better; we could be worse. There's no insurance policy.

POTTS: I gather that we can expect another book to pick up where *Parable of the Sower* left off.

BUTLER: Parable of the Talents is the book I am working on now.

POTTS: It will be interesting to see where you go with the story.

BUTLER: Well, in *Parable of the Sower* I focused on the problems—the things we have done wrong, that we appear to be doing wrong, and where those things can lead us. I made a real effort to talk about what could actually happen or is in the process of happening: the walled communities and the illiteracy and the global warming and lots of other things. In Parable of the Talents I want to give my characters the chance to work on the solutions, to say, "Here is the solution!"

POTTS: *Parable of the Sower* was published by a small press (Four Walls Eight Windows), as was your collection *Bloodchild and Other Stories*. *Kindred* was republished by a small press (Beacon). As a successful science fiction author, what made you turn to less commercial publishers?

BUTLER: I had probably reached some kind of plateau in science fiction, and I couldn't seem to get off it. I knew I had three audiences at least, but I couldn't get my science fiction publisher to pay any attention. I could tell them all day and all night, but they would answer, "Yes, that's right," and then go off and do something else. You know, the best way to defeat an argument is to agree with it and then forget about it. I had wanted to try one of the big publishers not normally associated with science fiction, and then my agent came up with this small publisher. I thought I would take the chance.

POTTS: Would you like to break down some of the walls between generic marketing categories?

BUTLER: Oh, that's not possible. You know how we are; if we kill off some, we will invent others.

POTTS: I ask in part because I noticed that Beacon Press published *Kindred* as a book in its Black Women Writers series.

BUTLER: Yes, I mentioned having three audiences: the science fiction audience, the Black audience, and the feminist audience.

POTTS: And being marketed through such categories doesn't trouble you.

BUTLER: Well, they're there, as I was just saying, and there's nothing you can do about it.

POTTS: I remember that during the New Wave of the sixties—

BUTLER: Oh, where is it now?

POTTS: —I was among those who believed that science fiction was moving to the forefront of literature.

BUTLER: Well, parts of it did move into the mainstream. In other cases, people simply did not call what they were doing "science fiction." I mean, Robin Cook did not announce that he was doing medical science fiction, and Dean Koontz does not publish his work as science fiction. And there are a lot of people who write science fiction although the word does not appear anywhere on the cover or inside. It doesn't mean they don't like science fiction; it means they want to make a good living.

POTTS: As I pointed out initially, your treatments of power, gender, and race coincide with many of the interests of current literary theory, and your own race and gender inevitably come into literary critiques of your work. Has being an African American woman influenced your choice of theme and approach?

BUTLER: I don't think it could do otherwise. All writers are influenced by who they are. If you are white, you could write about being Chinese, but you would bring in a lot of what you are as well.

POTTS: I cannot help noting—as you yourself observe in your essay "Positive Obsession"—that you are unique in the science fiction community. While there are more women working in the field than there were thirty years ago, there are few African Americans, and I still cannot think of another African American woman.

BUTLER: I have heard of some who have published stories. The ones who are actually writing books are not calling themselves science fiction authors, which is right because they are actually writing horror or fantasy. For instance, the woman who wrote the lesbian vampire stories, the Gilda stories, Jewelle Gomez—she's not science fiction but she is fantasy, and that's in the family. But I don't think she even presented her work as that.

POTTS: Do you think many people are still under the impression that science fiction is primarily a white male genre?

BUTLER: Yes. In fact, sometimes when I speak to general audiences, they are surprised there are a lot of women in science fiction. Because people do have a rather fixed notion of what science fiction is; it either comes from television or they pick it up somehow from the air, the ambience.

POTTS: Any last words to the science fiction critical community about how to approach your work?

BUTLER: Oh, good heavens, no!

POTTS: [*laughs*]

BUTLER: As far as criticism goes, what a reader brings to the work is as important as what I put into it, so I don't get upset when I am misinterpreted. Except when I say what I really meant was so-and-so, and I am told, "Oh, but subconsciously you must have meant this." I mean—leave me alone! [*laughs*] I don't mind attempts to interpret my fiction, but I am not willing to have critics interpret my subconscious. I doubt they are qualified.

POSSIBLE FUTURES

INTERVIEW BY CECILIA TAN
SOJOURNER
1999

"Feminism is freedom. It's the freedom to be who you are and not who someone else wants you to be. And science fiction? Science fiction is wide-open. You can go anywhere your imagination can go. Mainstream fiction isn't like that."

The author of a dozen groundbreaking novels, Octavia Butler is revered among three overlapping audiences: feminists, African American readers, and science fiction fans. Her first novel, *Patternmaster*, was published in 1976 and several novels in a related series soon appeared. Her most recent book series, begun with *Parable of the Sower* in 1994, was first published outside the science fiction genre by independent publisher Four Walls Eight Windows and promoted to feminist and African American bookstores and readers before being released in mass market paperback for the science fiction audience by Warner Aspect.

Butler's work examines issues of race, gender, class, and society as a whole in a way that only science fiction can, and her extraordinary vision has brought her a prestigious MacArthur "Genius" Grant. She describes herself as "a pessimist if I'm not careful, a feminist always, a Black, a quiet egoist, a former Baptist, and an oil-and-water combination of ambition, laziness, insecurity, certainty, and drive." But when asked in our recent interview if she sees herself as a visionary, she laughs.

OCTAVIA E. BUTLER: Good lord, no, that sounds so pompous. I don't see my role to be visionary. I'm a storyteller. I don't find my role to be anything in particular until I find myself doing it. Sometimes I don't know why an idea interests me or why something's rubbing me the wrong way [until the book is finished].

CECILIA TAN: Even so, would you say you spend a lot of time thinking about possible futures?

BUTLER: I just did a piece for *Essence* magazine for their thirtieth anniversary. I wound up writing about how to foretell the future rather than about what the future will be like. "Read history," [I said]. How can you foretell the future if you don't read history?

TAN: What do you think is going to happen to the human race in the next millennium?

BUTLER: Pretty much what is happening now. Why should anything different happen? There will be technological innovations and biological innovations, but things will be essentially how they are. The future is not some mystical magical place. The future is moment to moment. Thirty years ago we didn't have the computers we do now, but we're still doing the same things.

TAN: Meaning, even if the power grid collapses on January first, human beings are still going to be pretty much the same.

BUTLER: The human being is essentially lazy.

TAN: In your books, you often deal with issues of race and more general issues of stereotyping and the way pigeonholing people impedes social change.

BUTLER: It's all part of the same human laziness. We are prone to think in shorthand. It's like you're having an argument with someone and they suddenly decide, "Oh, you're a Malthusian," and dismiss your whole argument. Of course, the problem is that it works a lot of the time, and pigeonholing things helps us to deal more with the things we care about and less with the other. But it also prevents us from discovering things we could want to know. It's the way we are as human beings, and it has to be overcome again, and again, and again.

TAN: And you yourself suffered genre pigeonholing in your writing career. Is that what spurred you to publish with the independent presses like Beacon Press, Seven Stories Press, and Four Walls Eight Windows?

BUTLER: [In the 1980s] I had plateaued. It was hard for me to get published as anything other than science fiction, but I wasn't interested in scrabbling around for crumbs at the bottom of the genre. What I write is no more science fiction than *The Handmaid's Tale* but once people think of it as science fiction, you're stuck.

TAN: What did Four Walls Eight Windows do that big mass market publishers didn't?

BUTLER: Four Walls Eight Windows sent me on tour. I had never been on tour before, but I was willing to do whatever it took. Not a big long tour, but I got to ramble around the East Coast and a bit of the Midwest, Atlanta, New Orleans. I did talks at bookstores, and for media people, radio, print, some television. I am one of those people who looks hideous on television. I did book groups. That wasn't so much a part of the tour as people would find out I was going around and would invite me. I told the publisher I had potentially four audiences: the science fiction audience, the feminist audience, the Black audience, and maybe the New Age audience. He pretty much ignored the feminist angle until the feminist bookstores began to clamor, "Why isn't she coming here?" The tour was a good thing because people who had never heard of me could at least look at [the books] and decide for themselves whether they were interested in it, rather than having that decision made for them by genre division.

TAN: You write a lot about the future of society, but would you call your work utopian or dystopian? Pessimistic and cautionary, or meant to inspire?

BUTLER: I used to think of myself as pessimistic, but when working on *Adulthood Rites* I [changed my mind about that].

[Originally, I] wanted that book to end rather grimly and sadly. It's a middle book, and I wanted to give people a reason to read the third book. But I found the character took on a life of his own, developed a liking that surprised me, and took the story somewhere else entirely.

I have warned—the Parable novels are obviously novels of warning, cautionary tales. I have never written about a world I want to see develop—[although] maybe the Parable stories did that. I despair about the way we human beings injure ourselves and lay waste to the environment. The stupid things we do—we've always done them and chances are we always will, that's the kind of animals we are. This leaves me with the feeling that the kind of world I would like and that makes sense to me is not possible with the material we've got to work with.

In the Parable books, what I did was have my character offer a long-term goal backed by religion. Give people a goal that is backed by religion, and a plan that would last more than a generation, and it's not so much a way of making people better as a way of diverting their energies in a direction that would not be quite so negative (i.e., to go to the stars, to get to Heaven while you're still living)—this is the kind of project that will give people an outlet for their competitiveness and their desire to be important and things we don't always use to good effect. I can see it going wildly wrong. I can see us devastating this world in the effort to reach others, but that's the way my imagination works. Unhappily, that's one of the places things might lead, but my character has people practicing living in self-sufficient communities in the hope that it won't happen. I've been trying to fix humanity all along, but [the Parable books] are the first time I've tried to do it with the material at hand. Rather than with special powers, as in the Patternist books, it's just people using their own hands, their own brains.

TAN: What's the connection, for you, between feminism and science fiction?

BUTLER: Feminism is freedom. It's the freedom to be who you are and not who someone else wants you to be. I've noticed that the media has been pronouncing feminism dead for years, but then they have been pronouncing the novel dead for years. And science fiction? People ask me, "Why have you stuck with science fiction?" First of all, I say I'm not sure I have—I go wherever my imagination leads me. But second, science fiction is wide-open. You can go anywhere your imagination can go. Mainstream fiction isn't like that.

TAN: Freedom through fiction. I like that. Do you follow that old adage "write what you know"?

BUTLER: I prefer "write what you care about." One of the things about writing what you care about is you will be able to write about things for a long time. I rebelled against "write what you know" because that was what I was writing to get away from. What I knew was stultifying, but my imagination should be able to get out of that little box, even if my body couldn't.

TAN: What kinds of boxes have you left behind through writing?

BUTLER: The most fun I had—before the book I started recently—was the Xenogenesis books, [particularly *Imago*] because I had to create something that seemed to work but wasn't real. The odd family style was a part of it, a third sex person who really was a third sex person.

TAN: Do you think you'd stop writing if your dream for a sustainable future came true? Is the [technological] future already here?

BUTLER: The only thing that could keep me from writing is death or mental devastation. I don't write about the technological cutting edge—I tend to write about what people will be facing and how it will affect them, and how they will affect it.

TAN: What's next in Octavia Butler's future?

BUTLER: I'm fifty-two years old and have never moved to a place just because I wanted to. I'm moving to Seattle. I'm only here [in California] because I was afraid I'd have to take care of my mother. She passed on two years ago. I figure if I'm ever going to do it, I better do it.

In a way [moving] is like research for a book, because I had intended to write a book in which characters make a huge change. I'm not sure that will be my next book, but I want to save up my moving experiences for it, not just the experiences but the emotions, etc. Any kind of change that is big and expensive is somewhat scary.

I recently started a third Parable book, but I suspect I'm going to do something else in-between because it wasn't flowing. With Parable of the Trickster, what I have is an awful lot of furniture, but I don't have a lot of conflict. There are human problems, of course, but if you don't have a good conflict, you don't have a good story to tell, you don't have a plot.

I thought about doing a memoir, and I tried doing it, and it felt too much like stripping in public so I gave up. Either it would have to be dreadfully dull, or it would have been giving away things that don't altogether belong to me. My novels are the best of me. My novels and short stories are the best I have to offer. What I've done all my life is tell stories. Find the things I really care about and then tell the stories.

WATCHING THE STORY HAPPEN

INTERVIEW BY DARRELL SCHWEITZER
INTERZONE
APRIL 2002

In one sense, Octavia Butler is very easy to introduce. She is the author of *Wild Seed*, *Kindred*, *Clay's Ark*, the Xenogenesis novels, *Parable of the Sower*, *Parable of the Talents*, and several more of the most thoughtful and passionate novels in our field. She was born in 1947, sold her first story to the anthology Clarion edited by Robin Scott Wilson (having attended the Clarion [Science Fiction and Fantasy] Writers' Workshop) and published her first novel, *Patternmaster*, in 1976. She has attracted a good deal of critical attention. Other than that, all I can say is that in person she seems to be a quietly self-assured and unassuming person, the complete opposite of the sort of writer who cuts a flamboyant swath through a convention crowd and is the subject of countless anecdotes. You don't tell Octavia Butler stories. You read them—the ones she has written.

This interview was done at Eeriecon, in Niagara Falls, New York, April 21, 2002, where Octavia and I were both guests of honor, and was conducted in front of the convention as her guest-of-honor presentation.

DARRELL SCHWEITZER: To sort out your awards . . .

OCTAVIA E. BUTLER: I won a Nebula for "Bloodchild" and for the *Parable of the Sower*, and I won a Hugo for "Bloodchild" and "Speech Sounds."

SCHWEITZER: So you have an impressively stocked mantelpiece already.

BUTLER: I wish I had a mantel. It would be nice to put things up there. I just finally bought a house and it has no mantel. But it's funny to get three awards for my short stories when I'm essentially a novelist.

SCHWEITZER: But you must have started short.

BUTLER: I started writing short stories when I was very young. I started trying to sell them when [I] was thirteen. Fortunately nobody wanted to buy them. By the time I was able to sell anything, the first two things I sold were short stories, but thereafter I sold novels. "Thereafter" being five years later. I was one of the early Clarionites. I went to Clarion 1970. I sold two short stories, my very first sales, and I was so happy because then I knew I was a writer, and I would go home and write things, and people would buy them, and I'd be set for life. And it really hurt me when I didn't sell another word for five years.

SCHWEITZER: And one of those early stories was to have been in Last Dangerous Visions . . .

BUTLER: That is the one that you'll never see. Everybody knows about Last Dangerous Visions, I assume?

SCHWEITZER: It's sort of the Flying Dutchman of science fiction.

BUTLER: It's like, for a while I sort of hoped it would come out. Now, I'm really glad it didn't. Who wants their student work to come out twenty-five years later?

SCHWEITZER: You mentioned in the afterword to your story collection, *Bloodchild*, that when you were a kid and you were trying to write, your elder relatives were telling you, "Oh nonsense. You can't do this . . ."

BUTLER: It's kind of hard to convince people who came through the Depression the hard way that you're going to earn a living telling stories. What they're telling you is, "Grow up. Get a nice job with a salary and a pension." They couldn't figure out why I didn't think this was a good idea. I had a lot of jobs and I got to write about some of them later in *Kindred*. I gave them to my character. This is what writers do with their troubles and the unpleasantnesses of life. We give them to our characters. It makes them worthwhile. I quit all those jobs. I think the very last one, after I'd sold three novels and still had to do horrible little jobs, was working in a hospital laundry in August. Thoroughly unpleasant.

SCHWEITZER: In the afterword to *Bloodchild*, you talk about the need for persistence . . .

BUTLER: I'd done an essay on habits, good habits for would-be writers to establish. I said the most important one is persistence. That is also what I say when I am asked what talent I think is most important for a writer: just to keep at it until you finally do have some success. One of my favorite teachers, Harlan Ellison, used to say, "If anything can stop you from being a writer, don't be one." I suspect that goes without saying. There are so many things out there that are out to stop you. It's not a conspiracy or anything, but it's just so difficult to become a writer and live on your writing. So persistence is a good . . . "talent" may not be the right word . . . a good habit to develop.

SCHWEITZER: One thing I wanted to ask you about from the same afterword is where you said that persistence is more important than talent. I have certainly known wannabes who had every conceivable writerly virtue except talent. I know somebody who is a Clarion graduate, too, who has been beating his head against the wall for the past twenty-five years. He's never sold a word. I think he simply doesn't have it.

BUTLER: There may be another skill that he doesn't have, and that's learning from his mistakes. I remember having a Clarion student who told me she'd written something like eight unpublished novels. The problem was, she was good, but she would refuse to learn from her mistakes. She would just trash whatever it was and start again on something else. Your friend might be doing that. I justify saying that talent may be unimportant by suggesting that students go read the books on the bestseller list and see who else doesn't have any talent.

SCHWEITZER: Except for the celebrities who have the books ghosted for them, surely any published writer has to have a certain narrative ability?

BUTLER: You'd think so, wouldn't you. I've read some unbelievably poorly written stuff and I finally realized that good writing is just not a requirement, unfortunately.

SCHWEITZER: Let me bounce something off you. I have the Theory of Audience Starvation, which would account for a writer as bad as, say, James Fenimore Cooper, who, as you know, was just dreadful in every conceivable way, but he was writing about what the audience wanted to read about. If he had been writing conventional romances, set in Europe, he wouldn't have been publishable.

BUTLER: I agree. I have been reading romances recently. [*laughs*] Not the kind you're talking about, but I just wanted to see what's out there and why are people buying it. I realized that there is absolutely nothing in the books that is of any quality at all except the romance.

SCHWEITZER: It's got to have something the readers want. I'd suggest that if Tom Clancy wrote westerns, we'd never have heard of him. He came along at the time when the audience wanted techno-thrillers and he was competent enough to make himself intelligible.

BUTLER: He's also a decent storyteller, and that's important.

I think the most important thing a writer can do is tell a good story. If you don't do that, whatever else you do is liable not to be noticed.

SCHWEITZER: If you just write beautifully textured prose and there is no story, people will go to sleep after a while.

BUTLER: To me, that is what writer's block is. You're writing really well. You're getting nowhere. Hundreds of pages go by. Nothing much happens. To me, that's writer's block. I know, because I've been in the throes of one for a while, and I finally decided to quit what I was doing and write a nonfiction piece.

SCHWEITZER: Is that the unconscious telling you that the novel you're writing isn't ready yet?

BUTLER: Either that it isn't ready yet, or that it just isn't a novel. There's always that. I have an unpublished novel called Blindsight, which no one will ever see, except those few people who work for a certain publisher. It is no good because it doesn't go anywhere. I have a character and he does stuff, and that's pretty much it. I've got this blind psychic and he does stuff. Some of it is interesting stuff, but it doesn't really get anywhere in particular.

SCHWEITZER: Do you think you can come back to it someday and find the plot?

BUTLER: No. Some things just should be let alone, I think.

I rewrote it many times. This was on a manual typewriter. It was before computers. I rewrote it many times, and I'm done with it.

SCHWEITZER: Of course, if you become really famous, after you're dead they'll either publish it as a fragment or farm it out to somebody.

BUTLER: I hope not. It's what I said. It's not really worth publishing. I realize that someone might want to do it just for money. My heir, the person who will control things after I'm dead might very well do it, but I'll haunt her if she does.

SCHWEITZER: This has happened to any number of other writers. I recall how E. Hoffmann Price, in old age, burned certain things in self-defense.

BUTLER: I can't do it. I find it very difficult to get rid of things. I am a natural pack rat. My mother gave me this pack rat gene. It just means that when I'm dead there'll be so much junk that my cousin, who is my heir, will be just swimming in it. After a while she'll probably just give up and burn it all. Which won't be a bad thing.

SCHWEITZER: Or she could bring in vast quantities of scholars who will catalogue it all.

BUTLER: She doesn't have the patience.

SCHWEITZER: Is there a university already collecting your papers?

BUTLER: Actually there is. I'm willing them, not to a university, but to the Huntington Library because they asked for them and because Pasadena is my hometown. So whatever I put together and mark will go to them.

SCHWEITZER: Let's talk about the sciences you find interesting. A lot of the ones I've read have been based on biology, "Bloodchild," for instance. So, what attracts you to speculative biology?

BUTLER: No idea. I just follow my interests, and this has been an interest of mine for quite a long time. When I was in college I majored in quite a number of things for about five minutes each, and one of them was anthropology. I had the idea that I was going to be interested in cultural anthropology. Then I took that physical anthropology class and realized that what I was really interested in was evolutionary biology. I'm not interested in it enough to actually go and do something with it, but enough to read about and write about. I can't tell you why. It's just true. I do follow my interests. If something attracts me, especially if it won't let me alone, I am happy to write about it. Writers go through these periods of, you've got all these ideas and you're writing them, and then, after a while, you've written them, and you're refilling the well. I think I'm going through a period of refilling the well.

SCHWEITZER: Sprague de Camp used to say that as he got older, he had fewer ideas and so wrote more about them.

BUTLER: When I got the idea for *Patternmaster*, I was twelve years old. When I got the idea for *Mind of My Mind*, I was fifteen. I was nineteen when I got the idea for *Survivor*, which you won't see—and I hope you haven't already seen it, because it's bad—

SCHWEITZER: Is that the one you once described as your *Star Trek* novel?

BUTLER: Yeah, because the human beings go off to another world and immediately begin intermarrying with the natives, something that happens all the time on *Star Trek*.

SCHWEITZER: And they all wear jumpsuits and the landscape looks like Southern California . . . and then there's a shopping mall, right?

BUTLER: Not quite, but it's got its problems. But the reason I'm saying all this is that I got these ideas early on. I got the idea for *Kindred* while I was in college. This meant that when I finally began to sell, years later, I had all these ideas and I was working on them. They spawned other ideas. Then after a while, I'd written all that, and then I had to look around and see what else I wanted to do. That's when I wrote my Xenogenesis novels. I didn't know at first that there would be three of them, but I finally figured it out, three novels. It kind of worked out nicely. Then I got to the Parable books, and that was more difficult, because, well, they weren't something I'd lived with for a long time. It took me a while to get to the point of being able to write them. I had to get to know these characters. I had to get to know their world. I guess that's what I'm doing right now. I have several ideas. I have been writing at them. I've been writing several hundred pages of non-novel, and that's why I'm doing the nonfiction right now. It doesn't require me to be inspired, or anything else. It just requires me to do the research.

SCHWEITZER: What's the nonfiction?

BUTLER: It's a name book, which is all I want to say about it, and it's not a name dictionary. I'll say that. It's something I used to wish I had, and never found.

SCHWEITZER: Isn't that also the way one writes a novel?

BUTLER: In a sense, yes. When I started writing, one of the things I wanted to do was write myself in, because I was reading a lot of science fiction. I used to have a teacher who said, "Young science fiction writers read way too much science fiction." It was pretty much all I was reading. And I couldn't find me in there, so I wrote myself in.

SCHWEITZER: Did you have any perception at that time, as others have reported, that science fiction was supposed to be a man's game?

BUTLER: Not that. The nice thing about being an only child and a hermit is that I could imagine myself in all kinds of situations, and there was no one around to tell me I was being an idiot. And when my family finally did tell me I was an idiot, I didn't believe them, because by then I didn't believe them about much of anything.

SCHWEITZER: How did they react when you started publishing books?

BUTLER: They weren't impressed until I was able to quit that laundry job. No matter how many books you're publishing, if you're working at a hospital laundry, something's wrong . . . although I remember another writer and I corresponding, and he had dropped out. I said, "Why haven't I seen more from you?" He said, "Well, I didn't make anything on my first three books." My comment was, "Who makes anything on their first three books?" I remember that the time I quit that laundry job, it was to go to a Worldcon in Phoenix. Figure back to when that was. [1978—D.S.] I should have gotten more jobs, but I decided I was going to try to live as frugally as possible, and at that time you really could live very frugally. My rent was one-hundred dollars a month. So if you were content not to drive, and if you were content to wear the same clothes that you'd been getting along on for a long time . . . and there were other ways of not spending lots of money. I didn't eat potatoes for years after that. I decided that I was going to live off the writing, somehow. My next novel was *Kindred*, which I didn't want to sell to Doubleday, because I got the same amount for the first three Doubleday books, and that same amount was

$1,750. Even then, that wasn't a lot of money. So I wanted to get more for *Kindred*, which I felt really was my best work to that time. And I wound up shopping it all over the place, and I ended up taking it back to Doubleday.

No one else wanted to take a chance on it, because nobody knew what it was. It didn't quite qualify as science fiction. It didn't qualify as anything else, really. They didn't know what it was, so they didn't want it, and so I wound up in the Doubleday trade department. I got a little more money and used it to hire myself a publicist, and I began to do a bit better.

SCHWEITZER: Now you're doing a lot better, it would seem. Your books are in a lot of stores, unlike those Doubleday books, which doubtless disappeared instantly and became fabulous collector's items.

BUTLER: Yes. People pay a lot of money for them now. Oh well . . . [*laughs*] I still have some of them, so, who knows? They're kind of part of my retirement.

SCHWEITZER: What is the genesis of the two Parable books? These are a bit of a departure . . .

BUTLER: No, they're not, really. They're another case of me trying to fix the world, trying to fix the human species. We seem so likely to destroy ourselves. We work so hard at doing things which will harm us. I figure that if we ever do die out as a species, it will be because of something we did, as opposed to the asteroid striking, or something.

I keep trying to find ways to fix us. In the Xenogenesis books, genetic engineering. In the earlier books, mental abilities, telepathy, that kind of thing. In the Parable books, I made a rule: no aliens, no powers, no humanity-altering genetic engineering, just what we've got to work with. So people have to find a way, using the tools we've got. The tool my character chooses is religion. It's not really different; it's just going at the same thing in a different way.

SCHWEITZER: I've heard you speak elsewhere and describe gloomy prognostications for the future, what you refer to as "the Burn." Could you describe that?

BUTLER: That's just something I was working on for the Parable books. It was renamed "the Apocalypse," then shortened to "the Pox." The Pox is the nasty part of history that happens as a result of all the problems that we're neglecting now, from illiteracy to drugs to global warming, that are likely to give us trouble in the future just because we're ignoring them now. Today's troubles that grow up into tomorrow's disasters. Unfortunately, a lot of them mature at the same time. That's "the Pox." It's supposed to be something that we're already working on. It's already happening now. It comes to maturity in the 2020s.

SCHWEITZER: Here we are in Niagara Falls in mid-April and it's eighty degrees out. It was ninety in Philadelphia.

BUTLER: We can enjoy it . . .

SCHWEITZER: We can, but when I was a kid, we had spring.

BUTLER: I remember being on a television program in Chicago where high school children were allowed to ask questions, and somebody got me talking about global warming. And the other person on the program said, "It's nothing really to worry about." I asked, "How can you say that?" He said that getting warmer is just not that much of a problem. It's been warmer than we're likely to get. Why worry about it? Of course it has, but not while we were around with all our cities built on coastlines. I think that that attitude of "it's nothing to worry about," and the tendency to treat each incident that might relate to global warming as a separate incident, is one of the things that is liable to get us to something very like "the Pox."

SCHWEITZER: You could buy beachfront property five hundred miles inland from New Orleans . . .

BUTLER: I've just moved from Southern California to Seattle. In 1999, I did that. I think I believe a little bit of what I've been saying.

SCHWEITZER: Do you think that writing novels about this has much impact?

BUTLER: Not now, no. Not enough people are suffering. I do think novels and movies and TV shows had an impact on whether or not we had that thermonuclear war. I think novels and films matter when people begin to get frightened, because then novels help them to imagine possibilities, that maybe they don't want to imagine, but they need to.

SCHWEITZER: There's a great Ray Bradbury line, that the purpose of science fiction is not to predict the future, but to prevent it.

BUTLER: Perhaps to give warning. There's an old idea that science fiction has the three categories, the "What If," "If Only," and "If This Goes On." The Parable books are definitely an "If This Goes On" story.

SCHWEITZER: If we are to be a little more pessimistic, I would think that a religion that would come out of a crisis like "the Burn" would be a really militant, nasty one.

BUTLER: It could be. In fact, a nasty one does come out. But there's also my characters' religion. I grew up, had my adolescence during the space race.

I used to get up at three or four in the morning and watch the space shots go. It seemed to me that that was our way of having that nuclear war without having it. We were able to get the technological boost. We were able to compete with our enemies, and we were able not to kill a good portion of the human species in the process. I thought about that, when I created Earthseed, the religion of my character. I thought, what might she propose as a goal that might be worth going after, but that wouldn't involve wiping out a good portion of humanity? What I thought of was the idea of going to the stars. It is such a huge, difficult, long-term family of projects that it just might hold our attention, give us the boost we need, especially when it comes as a religious mandate. It could also cause a lot of trouble. It probably would, considering that we human beings are good at finding things to fight about, making trouble where it isn't necessary. But I had my character persist and manage to at least get people started.

SCHWEITZER: Are you optimistic or pessimistic toward the future? Utopia, disaster, or do we just somehow muddle through?

BUTLER: I don't know. The problem is that we're really good at responding to crises, but we're really bad at long-term planning, especially when it requires that we stop doing something that we really enjoy doing, like burning fossil fuels. Probably we will muddle through for a while, but sooner or later we'll push the environment too far. We'll do something that we won't be able to recover from.

SCHWEITZER: Indeed, if we ever did have that thermonuclear war, it might not be possible to build civilization again, because, among other things, all the easily obtainable fuel and metals have already been mined out and you have to have high technology to extract what's left.

BUTLER: Or we might have to do something else. Our inventiveness is not something that I have a problem with. It is our tendency not to plan far enough ahead. We might see the cliff. I don't drive. I am one of the few people I know who lived in Los Angeles for most of my life who doesn't drive. The reason I don't drive is that I'm a bit dyslexic. I have fairly quick reactions, but they're strange. When I was learning to drive, my teacher had me on a little mountain road, a two-lane road where you really had to squeeze past another car, and I was headed out on this little windy road, and I realized that I had to turn. Left and right mean nothing to me. You can say, "Go left," and if my life depends on it, I'm liable to go right. So the teacher wanted me to go a certain way, and it was obvious that I should because the other way was off a cliff. Well, I didn't process what he said and I went the wrong way. If there had not been dual controls on the car, I wouldn't be here. I think, sometimes, there is a problem like that with the human species.

We might see the right way, but we don't do it, not because we're dyslexic, but because we just find it more comfortable or more financially rewarding to go the wrong way, at least as long as we can.

AUDIENCE: Are you going to write more of the Parable books?

BUTLER: Not with the same main character, because she's dead. I had the idea of following two or four groups who leave. There's a verse in the character's religion that says, "God is teacher, trickster, chaos, clay." I was going to do The Parable of the Trickster, The Parable of the Teacher, The Parable of Chaos, and The Parable of Clay. It didn't work out. I still might do them, but I'm not doing them now. As a matter of fact, the fiction I am working on now, or that I was working on before I went to the nonfiction book, is an odd fantasy that I suddenly came up with because I used to know a very interesting lady that I've never been able to use in a story before. She's found her way into this one.

SCHWEITZER: It sounds like you've been hit by lightning several times during your career, and have spent the rest of your life writing that out.

BUTLER: Everybody is.

SCHWEITZER: Everybody is, but most people don't recognize it and do anything with it.

BUTLER: It's more lighting, really. I wait until there's something that won't let me alone. I don't always wait. Sometimes I dive right in too quickly. But, best case, I wait until something won't let me alone, either because I agree, or I disagree with it, or because it fascinates me.

SCHWEITZER: What I mean by being hit by lightning is a case like Bram Stoker. He spent most of his life as a theatrical manager, but he still cranked out a number of routine books. He got hit by lightning once, and wrote *Dracula*, and nothing else he did mattered.

BUTLER: I am a little bothered by your putting it that way. I understand what you mean. It's one of the things that I try to keep young writers from thinking, that you have to wait, that it's all luck, lightning will strike and then you'll have a wonderful bestseller. So I think it's like the old idea that fortune favors the prepared mind. If you've developed the habit of paying attention to the things that happen around you and to you, then, yeah, you'll get hit by lightning.

SCHWEITZER: I think that you should tell the young writers to write up every story they feel like writing, because you only know in retrospect and possibly years later, if you were ever hit by lightning.

BUTLER: I don't think so. You'd waste an awful lot of time writing crap.

SCHWEITZER: True, but to use the example of Stoker, did he know that *Dracula* was head and shoulders above everything else he ever wrote, when he wrote it, or did he only discover this long afterwards?

BUTLER: On the other hand, did he write every thought he had?

SCHWEITZER: He probably didn't have time to. He had a very busy life.

AUDIENCE: Classical music is classic music because it has survived beyond its marketing age. The stuff that you don't hear anymore, maybe you don't hear because it wasn't so good . . .

BUTLER: Maybe it just didn't have the necessary PR.

AUDIENCE: Maybe the rest of Bram Stoker's books weren't very good.

BUTLER: But I don't think this is something you should worry about. I remember being on a panel at a science fiction convention years ago, and one of the questions put to us was, "How do you want to be remembered?" And I said, "Forget remembered. I just want to be read now." Everybody else had been talking about how they wanted to be remembered and which books they wanted to be remembered for. We don't have any control over that. It's not something that I worry about. I guess that's what I mean, too. You really can't decide, "Well, I'm going to write everything because something might be a wonderful hit." It's not something you can control.

AUDIENCE: [question about youthful writing]

BUTLER: What I wrote when I was ten should have been put in the garbage. But, to tell the truth, I still have it all. The good thing is that it was written in #2 pencil on both sides of the page, so it's illegible now. It rubbed off on itself. But I didn't know how to write a novel when I was twelve years old, when I got the idea for *Patternmaster*. I didn't know how to write a novel when I was twenty. I didn't learn how to write a novel until I hit bottom, in a work-related way. I was, as I said, taking a lot of horrible jobs, and I took a job as a telemarketer. At that time it was called "telephone solicitation." I have a good phone voice. I am told I have a good phone presence, and I actually sold things to people. I'm very ashamed. But mostly I would call them, bother them, and they'd cuss me out. I'd call someone else . . . This is why I don't cuss telephone marketers. I just quietly hang up on them. I got laid off that job about two weeks before Christmas, back in the seventies. Any job that you get laid off two weeks before Christmas, this is a kind of disaster. I knew it wasn't going to be a very good Christmas. I actually cried about losing that job. If I was crying about losing a job that awful, it was definitely time to fish or cut bait. It was time for me either to write the novels, or get that civil service job that my mother had been urging on me, the one with the pension. Still, though, I didn't know how to write a novel. No idea. So I thought about what I had written. I realized that I did know how to write a short story. My short stories averaged about twenty pages long. I thought that twenty pages might be fairly decent for a novel chapter, and the way I wrote my first novels was in twenty-page increments. I was very lucky that my first novel, *Patternmaster*, was a kind of chase story, because chase stories have built-in endings. I didn't know at the time that I needed an end, before I began. If I didn't have an end, I wouldn't get anywhere. I'd just wander. I had been wandering, but when this version of *Patternmaster* became a chase story, this plan worked. I think of it as a method of novel writing, twenty pages at a time. That's how I managed to get my first stuff done. I did *Patternmaster*, mailed it out, did *Mind of My Mind*, mailed it out, got busy on the version of *Survivor* that was eventually published, and was about halfway through it before I had to go back to work.

AUDIENCE: How did you find research materials for *Wild Seed*?

BUTLER: I was very lucky. I had the Los Angeles Public Library, the main branch nearby. In some cases, it would have one copy of something that looked like it had been mimeographed. I wasn't allowed to take it out of the room. So I had to use their copier, fifteen cents a page, and pretty much photocopy the thing. There were others that I was allowed to check out, special-loan. I was able to do all the research I had to do at the library, mainly because I had no money. I couldn't afford to go to Nigeria. I couldn't even afford to go to upstate New York. I had just finished *Kindred*, and I was in a kind of depression. It was hard to write and not pleasant to research—that was the real research job, by the way—and *Kindred* wasn't selling. And I just drowned my sorrows in writing *Wild Seed*. It was fun, to my surprise. Shortly after that, somebody torched the Los Angeles Public Library and a lot of the stuff that I only got to see disappeared forever. So I was lucky, in that case. I had a lot of good stuff available. Why anybody would torch a library, I still don't know.

HAL CLEMENT (FROM AUDIENCE): People have been burning individual books for a long time.

BUTLER: I don't think they ever found out who did it. I blame the city council, myself. They knew that it was a firetrap, and for years they had done nothing. Remodeling was supposed to be finally about to start after years of, "Well, we can save money by not doing this, so let's not do it. We'll proclaim ourselves wonderful savers of the taxpayers' money. And then when it finally gets burned, oh well . . ." The way it burned,

I'm not sure what to make of that. The fire began in religion and burned directly up to science, then over to social science, where there was a lot more water damage than fire damage. Somebody maybe thought this one out.

SCHWEITZER: This is what they mean by "intelligent design."

BUTLER: I hope not.

AUDIENCE: How do you go about plotting a novel which is essentially character driven, as opposed to action driven?

BUTLER: There's plenty of action in *Wild Seed*, but I know what you mean. I had to, because I wrote the end before the beginning. I wrote *Mind of My Mind*, and it was published, and writing *Wild Seed* was writing a prequel to *Mind of My Mind*. There was a real limit to what I could do. That was another kind of puzzle. I discovered, to my amazement, that I liked puzzles. I never thought I did, when I was in school. But I guess I like the puzzles that I choose or create. Okay, I have these two people and I know how they turn out. So, what can I do with them? That's what I had to figure out. It was writing in a box, and I really enjoyed solving the problem. How I did it? It's been a long time, but I find that I don't like to outline. Outlining to me kills the immediacy of the story. I guess what I mean by that is the more detailed outline. I have to know where I'm headed. I had to have that before I began the story. I had to tell myself the story in a sentence, although the sentence that describes that novel is not a good one. This just meant, "How do I get from here to there?" and what kind of divisions, time periods, where do I want to head, and how far do I want to go with it. Sometimes history provides you with a kind of outline.

AUDIENCE: One thing I've always liked about the Patternist universe series, is that it is so obviously a complete universe, planned out.

BUTLER: I never really planned *Clay's Ark* when I began those books, but when I'd written *Patternmaster* and *Mind of My Mind*, I realized that I did want to know more about the Clayarks, and I began asking myself questions. That's when I came up with the book *Clay's Ark*. I used to live in the desert of Southern California, so I have been wanting to set a book out there for a long time. I think I got the idea for how to do it when I was on my way home from that Worldcon I mentioned. I had been in Phoenix, and I was taking a Greyhound bus home. I used to ride Greyhound buses all over the country. Ever so much fun. And there was a storm. First it was a sand and dust storm, where you could barely see anything. Then it rained, and it was a mud storm, where you absolutely couldn't see anything. Sensible people were pulled over to the side of the road because they couldn't see. But Greyhound bus drivers have schedules. The bus kept on going. All I could think was, the driver didn't look suicidal, so probably he wanted to live. He must have been able to see something. I finally figured out that he could see the yellow line, which didn't really seem to be enough, but that storm is the beginning of *Clay's Ark* as well as an interesting facet of my life.

SCHWEITZER: Do you avoid outlining in detail because the books are a process of discovery, that you only discover what's in them by writing them?

BUTLER: Yeah. I do need to know, as I said, the end. Maybe it's a process of discovering how to get there.

SCHWEITZER: Do you ever get to the end and discover it wasn't the end you thought?

BUTLER: No, but I had a case where I discovered in the middle that I wasn't going to the end I thought I was. That was *Adulthood Rites*, which is the middle book of a trilogy. I thought it was going to be a downbeat book with a really bad, cliff-hanger ending—bad in the sense that my characters would be in big trouble. But it came to a completely different sort of ending because my character insisted on finding a way to save some of what was left of humankind. Once I realized that was where he was headed, I just let him go and watched the story happen. It was fun to write.

"I'VE ALWAYS BEEN AN OUTSIDER"

INTERVIEW BY JOSHUNDA SANDERS
INMOTION MAGAZINE
FEBRUARY 2004

This is how Octavia Butler described herself, the first self-possessed Black woman writer introvert, I had the honor of writing about for publication. Actually interviewing her was one of the great honors of my life, two years before her death in 2006. I wonder what she would have made of this beautiful Google Doodle, which I was delightfully surprised to see this morning before I went to sleep.

I was twenty-six when I interviewed her, and Octavia Butler was the first person of consequence who was meaningful to the culture that I would interview. That year, I would also meet my mentor, and interview other influential Black women writers and scholars who inspired me to keep writing, even if they may not have been aware that's what they were doing in the moment.

What I found most delightful about Octavia Butler was how unimpressed she was with herself and her habits. She had so many gifts that she shared with us, and so much wisdom. Our elders can see ahead on the path, can keep us from making mistakes we don't need to.

I'll always be so grateful for how generously kind she was with me, even though I was so clearly new at interviewing writers. I greatly respected how she wove stories even when she was talking about the most mundane things—we were discussing her first visit to New York, for instance, when she described the stamina you need to do something physical as akin to the writing life: "I think climbing mountains or buildings or whatever has been a really good metaphor for finishing my work. Because no matter how tired you get, no matter how you feel like you can't possibly do this, somehow you do."

Even if our culture only values what we can see at this moment, what they offer us is information about coping with the hard things in life—in the past, in what they imagined the future to be—that can tell us much more than any anxiety might be able to.

Octavia Butler is one of the few African American women writing in the male-dominated science fiction genre. The worlds she creates with her pen are groundbreaking, powerful multicultural revisions of history; sometimes frightening and complex visions of the future. The author of twelve books and an award-winning collection of short stories, Butler was also the recipient of an esteemed MacArthur Fellowship grant in 1995—the only science fiction writer on a list of more than six hundred names in the last twenty years. She's also won the most esteemed awards in the genre: the Hugo and Nebula Awards for her books and short stories.

While she has referred to herself simply by saying, "I'm Black. I'm solitary. I've always been an outsider," Butler, fifty-six, manages to render the emotional lives of her characters like an insider. It is a talent that she attributes to her life's journey—she challenges her readers to confront themselves in spite of their circumstances and often, because of them.

The only living child of a shoeshine man and a maid who grew up a bookworm and loner in Pasadena, California, has crafted the universe according to Octavia Estelle Butler since she was four; though she didn't start making a living at it until she was older. Before she embarked on a professional writing career, she took writing classes, did odd jobs—from telemarketing to sorting potato chips—before she sold her first novel, *Patternmaster*, in 1976. Currently, she is on tour, celebrating the twenty-fifth anniversary of the publication of *Kindred*— the story of a modern day woman who is transported back to the antebellum South to save her white ancestor. Her most recent works are two short stories titled "The Book of Martha" and "Amnesty."

JOSHUNDA SANDERS: You grew up in Pasadena, California? What made you want to move to Seattle?

OCTAVIA E. BUTLER: I went to Seattle for the first time in 1976. My first novel was published then, and that meant that I could take my first vacation. I got on a Greyhound bus and took a Greyhound Ameripass tour, which means that for a month I could go wherever I wanted to on Greyhound. There were a lot more buses then, so it was nice. Now I'm not sure it would be, because they get into so many places in the middle of the night and they leave in the middle of the night. So, it's kind of inconvenient. But anyway, I went to Seattle, among other places. I went first to New York, because I'd never been there and I wanted to go.

SANDERS: What'd you think of New York?

BUTLER: I had a great time there. I met this West Indian woman, we were both going to the Statue of Liberty. She was wearing these thick-soled sandals, really uncomfortable shoes. We were both going to go to the top of the Empire State Building. Now, with me, my only excuse is that I'm not in shape, and wasn't then. And with her, it was her feet. We'd encourage each other back and forth going to the top. And finally made it.

I think climbing mountains or buildings or whatever has been a really good metaphor for finishing my work. Because no matter how tired you get, no matter how you feel like you can't possibly do this, somehow you do.

I hiked down not quite to the bottom of the Grand Canyon because I only had that one day, it was part of the same trip. I discovered that I didn't really like going to cities, so I went to national parks. And I hiked almost to the bottom and I realized that the bus was going to leave me if I didn't get myself back up. Now it's easy going down, but coming back up . . . and I did it completely unprepared. So, I didn't have any water . . . this is not sensible and I don't think anyone should do it. I didn't have anything except maybe some candies like this [*she holds up a peppermint candy*] because they tend to live at the bottom of my bag. And I kept thinking, "How embarrassing, and how humiliating it would be if somebody had to come get me." I mean, it really hurts to walk that much if you're out of shape and not used to it.

SANDERS: Why did you think you could do it?

BUTLER: It never occurred to me. I didn't know what I was doing. I mean, it was a totally silly thing to do. And I kept trying and I would push myself. Part way down and part way back the only water was when it began to rain. And then it began to rain sideways and it plastered mud all down the front of my body. But I got back up on my own two feet, which really hurt by the time I got back up. And it's sort of like writing.

When I went to Peru, I climbed Huayna Picchu, the taller of the two peaks you see when you see Machu Picchu. It's an easy climb for anyone who is okay, you know. I mean, even if you're not in very good shape. But I managed to hurt my knee hiking. I kept saying, this is high enough, this is high enough, why don't I go back down? I got all the way to the top, crawled through the little cave and got to the top of the mountain and came back down. That's what I mean. It's a good metaphor for writing, because there will always come a time in writing a novel for instance, a long undertaking like that, when you don't think you can do it. Or, you think it's so bad you want to throw it away. I tell the students that there comes a time when you want to either burn it or flush it. But if you keep going, you know, that's what makes you a writer instead of an "I wish I was a writer."

I had a dentist when I was down in Pasadena and he knew I wrote and I had given him a couple of my books. And his attitude then was, "Well, writing is so easy even she can do it, so I'll do some writing." And he wrote the most appalling piece of . . . well. Truly bad. And he gave it to me to read. And I should have said, well, for legal reasons I don't want to read your work, but I did him a favor and read his work. But what I had to say about it, as gently as I could say it, was, "Let this be an exercise, go take a class, here are some of the problems you might want to work on." Very gently. But I never really wanted to let him at me with a drill again after that. So it cost me a dentist. But that was his attitude, you know, if I was doing it, it must be easy and anybody could do it.

SANDERS: A lot of people have that attitude about writing, but one of the things that strikes me about your work in particular is that it's so complex that I don't understand how people could come to you with that sort of cavalier attitude.

BUTLER: I don't think they see it that way. I think their attitude has more to do with me than with the work. Just me, as a Black, as a woman, or as a woman who doesn't look as though she could do anything terribly complex.

SANDERS: That doesn't frustrate you?

BUTLER: Oh, I'm doing okay.

SANDERS: What is it that fascinates you about books?

BUTLER: My big problem is my mother gave me this gene— there must be a gene for it, or several perhaps. It's the pack rat gene, you know, where you just don't throw things out. I haven't thrown books out since I was a kid. I gave some books away when I was a little girl. My mother said I could give some to the Salvation Army. I gave some to a friend, and her brothers and sisters tore them [to] bits. That was the last time I gave books away in large amounts. I just keep stuff. I still have books from childhood.

SANDERS: That's a blessing.

BUTLER: It comforts me. I imagine when I'm dead someone will have a huge yard sale or estate sale and I don't care! Some of them are worth something. Even my comic books—I have first editions of this and that, the first issue of the Fantastic Four. I used to collect them, not in the way that people collect things now. I didn't put them in plastic bags and never touch them. I read them and they looked pretty bad, some of them. But they're still worth something just because they are what they are.

SANDERS: How has your childhood affected your work?

BUTLER: I think writers use absolutely everything that happens to us, and surely if I had had a different sort of childhood and still come out a writer, I'd be a different kind of writer. It's on a par with, but different from, the fact that I had four brothers who were born and died before I was born. Some of them didn't come to term, some of them did come to term and then died. But my mother couldn't carry a child to term, for the most part something went wrong. If they had lived, I would be a very different person. So, anything that happens in your life that is important, if it didn't happen you would be someone different.

SANDERS: People attach a lot of titles to you—

BUTLER: Please don't call me the grande dame. Someone said it in *Essence* and it stuck.

SANDERS: You're annoyed by it?

BUTLER: Well, it's another word for grandmother! I'm certainly old enough to be someone's grandmother, but I'm not.

SANDERS: What about the science fiction or speculative fiction titles attached to your work?

BUTLER: Really, it doesn't matter. A good story is a good story. If what I'm writing reaches you, then it reaches you no matter what title is stuck on it. The titles are mainly so that you'll know where to look in the library, or as a marketing title, know where to put it in the bookstore so booksellers know how to sell it. It has very little to do with actual writing.

SANDERS: Have you found that it intimidates African Americans, in particular?

BUTLER: No. I think people have made up their minds that they don't like science fiction because they've made up their minds that they know what science fiction is. And they have a very limited notion of what it is. I used to say science fiction and Black people are judged by their worst elements. And it's sadly enough still true. People think, "Oh, science fiction, *Star Wars*. I don't like that." And they don't want to read what I've written because they don't like *Star Wars*. Then again, you get the other kind who do want to read what I've written because they like *Star Wars* and they think that must be what I'm doing. In both cases they're going to be disappointed. That's the worst thing about verbal shorthand. All too often, it's an excuse not to do something, more often than it's a reason for doing something.

There isn't any subject you can't tackle by way of science fiction. And probably there isn't any subject that somebody hasn't tackled at one time or another. You don't have the formulas that you might have for a mystery, or even a romance. It's completely wide-open. If you're going to write science fiction, that means you're using science and you'll need to use it accurately. At least speculate in ways that make sense, you know. If you're not using science, what you're probably writing is fantasy, I mean if it's still odd. Some species of fantasy . . . people tend to think fantasy, oh Tolkien, but *Kindred* is fantasy because there's no science. With fantasy, all you have to do is follow the rules that you've created.

SANDERS: There are so many parts of the Parables, for instance, that seem to echo what's happening in the world right now.

BUTLER: Keep in mind that when I wrote them, Bush wasn't president. Clinton had yet to be reelected. When I wrote them the time was very different. I was trying not to prophesize. Matter of fact, I was trying to give warning.

One of the kinds of research I did was to read a lot of stuff about World War II. Not the war itself, but I wanted to know in particular how a country goes fascist. So, I have this country, in *Parable of the Sower*, and especially *Parable of the Talents*, sliding in that direction. And I really was not trying to prophesize that somehow we would do that but . . .

SANDERS: Is it jarring to you, with the new mission to Mars and such?

BUTLER: Oh, no, I don't see any reason to pay attention to that. I don't think Bush is any more serious about Mars than he was about getting rid of some of our emissions in the atmosphere. It's just something he said and probably forgot it a moment later. Or will eventually. Because, after all, it's not something that's supposed to happen while he's still in office. It can't. So I don't think we need to really pay any attention to that.

SANDERS: You came of age when there was an actual space race, but my generation is a little removed from that.

BUTLER: I think of the space race as a way of having a nuclear war without having one. I mean that literally. We had a competition with the USSR and from that competition came a lot of good technical fallout. We learned a lot of things we hadn't known before, even things that apply to weapons systems, and yet we didn't wipe each other out. I mean, there were people who thought a nuclear war would be a cool idea. During the early part of the Reagan era, there were people who thought we could win a nuclear war and rid ourselves of the Soviet Empire. I thought they were nuts, but they were there. And Reagan got into office in spite of the fact that he thought a nuclear war was winnable.

SANDERS: That's heavy stuff.

BUTLER: I got my idea for the Xenogenesis books (*Dawn, Adulthood Rites* and *Imago*) from Ronald Reagan because he was advocating this kind of thing. I thought there must be something basic, something really genetically wrong with us if we're falling for this stuff. And I came up with these characteristics. The aliens arrive after the war and they tell us that we have these two characteristics that don't work and play well together. They are intelligent, and they tell us we're the most intelligent species they've come across. But we're also hierarchical. And I put this after the big war because it's kind of an example. We've one-upped ourselves to death, just our tendency to one-up each other as individuals and groups, large and small.

It has a greater consequence if you combine it with intelligence. If what you have is two elk fighting over who's going to make the food, I mean, the consequences to them . . . but if you're going to have somebody sending people off to war for egotistical or economic reasons, both hierarchal sorts of reasons, you end up with a lot more dead people. When you're throwing nuclear weapons in the pie, which is what we were doing back then, you end up with more dead people than any war before. It could have been very bad.

SANDERS: Do some of your ideas disturb you or keep you up at night?

BUTLER: A lot of the ones in the Parables, of course, did. Like I said, they weren't things that I wanted to happen. *Kindred* was a difficult book to write because of the research I had to do. The slave narratives, the histories in general—I read books written by the wives of plantation owners, at the LA Public Library. Unfortunately, a few years after that, somebody torched it. Some of the books I used to write *Wild Seed* and *Kindred*, they would have been one copy in the library and now they're gone.

SANDERS: Why do you think *Kindred* has been one of your more popular works?

BUTLER: Because it's accessible to a number of audiences: Black studies, oh, I guess I have to modify my vocabulary here—African American studies, women's studies and science fiction. It sometimes reaches people who might not otherwise read that kind of book, who might not read a history, a historical novel even about that period unless it was a *Gone with the Wind* type.

[With *Kindred*] I chose the time I was living in. I thought it was interesting to start at the bicentennial and the country's two-hundred years old and the country's still dealing with racial problems, and here's my character having to deal with slavery all of a sudden. If I had written the book now, it probably wouldn't be very different. What I was trying to do is make the time real, I wanted to take them back into it. The idea was always to make that time emotionally real to people. And that's still what it's about. The nice thing is that it is read in schools. Every now and then I hear about younger kids reading it and I wonder how they relate to it. All too often, especially young men, will feel, "Oh, if it was me, I would just . . ." and they have some simple solution that wouldn't work at all and would probably get them killed. Because they don't really understand how serious it is when the whole society is literally arrayed against you and arrayed to really keep you in your place. If you get seriously out of line, they will kill you because they fear you.

Kindred was kind of draining and depressing, especially the research for writing it. I now have a talk that begins with the question, "How long does it take to write a novel?" and the answer is, as long as you've lived up to the time you sit down to write the novel and then some. I got the idea for it in college. But a lot of my reason for writing it came when I was in preschool, when my mother used to take me to work with her.

I got to see her not hearing insults and going in back doors, and even though I was a little kid, I realized it was humiliating. I knew something was wrong, it was unpleasant, it was bad. I remember saying to her a little later, at seven or eight, "I'll never do what you do, what you do is terrible." And she just got this sad look on her face and didn't say anything. I think it was the look and the memory of the indignities she endured. I just remembered that and wanted to convey that people who underwent all this were not cowards, were not people who were just too pathetic to protect themselves, but were heroes because they were using what they had to help their kids get a little further. She knew what it was to be hungry, she was a young woman during the Depression; she was taken out of school when she was ten. There were times when there was no food, there were times when they were scrambling to put a roof over their heads. I never had to worry about any of that. We never went hungry, we never went homeless. I got to go to college and she didn't even get to finish elementary school. All that because she was willing to put up with this nonsense and try to help me. I wanted to convey some of that and not have it look as though these people were deficient because they weren't fighting. They were fighting, they just weren't fighting with fists, which is sometimes easy and pointless. The quick and dirty solution is often the one that's most admired until you have to live with the results.

SANDERS: So I hear you're working on a book about a vampire?

BUTLER: It's sort of like my *Wild Seed* for this time in my life. I wrote *Wild Seed* as my reward for having written *Kindred*. I wrote the two Parable books and I was trying to write a third, and I wasn't getting anything worthwhile done. To me, writer's block doesn't mean that I can't write—it just means that what I'm writing is not worth anything and that writing it is difficult and unpleasant. And then, for some reason I got hold of a vampire story and it was a lot of fun, I really enjoyed it. And after a while, I found myself writing one. It's a novel, I'm enjoying it and I hope other people will, too.

SANDERS: Where do you get your ideas?

BUTLER: When I got the idea for *Patternmaster*, I was twelve, but I had no idea how to write a novel. I tried, but it was quite a few years before I was able to write it. When I got the idea for *Mind of My Mind*, I was fifteen. When I got the idea for *Survivor*, I was nineteen. Finally, when I got the idea for *Kindred*, I was in college. My ideas generally come from what's going on around me. But sometimes they come from other novels. For instance, when I wrote *Patternmaster*, I included these people called the Clayarks and they were just kind of throwaway people, but I didn't like them as throwaway people and I wanted to know more about them. So I wrote *Clay's Ark*. And learned about them as I went along. Sometimes a book will seem like one book and turn into two or three, which happened with the Xenogenesis books. Sometimes I hear from people who want to write and [they ask] what should they do? The first thing I want to know from them is, are they writing? Are they writing every day? And a remarkable number of them are not. Do they read omnivorously, because that's not only a source of ideas, but a way to learn to write, to see what other people have been up to. I recommend that they take classes because it's a great way to rent an audience and make sure you're communicating what you think you're communicating, which is not always the case, and I recommend that they forget a couple of things. Forget about talent. I recommend that they go to the best-selling lists and see who else doesn't have talent and it hasn't stopped them, so don't worry. Forget about inspiration, because it's more likely to be a reason not to write, as in, "I can't write today because I'm not inspired." I tell them I used to live next to my landlady and I told everybody she inspired me. And the most valuable characteristic any would-be writer can possibly have is persistence. Just keep at it, keep learning your craft and keep trying.

INTERVIEWING THE ORACLE

INTERVIEW BY KAZEMBE BALAGUN
THE INDYPENDENT
JANUARY 13, 2006

Octavia Butler's conversation style is like her prose: lean and to the point. Not that she does not have a lot to talk about. She has written eleven novels including *Kindred*, whose heroine keeps falling back in time to save her white slave master ancestor, and *Parable of the Sower*, a richly imagined tale of a small band of survivors founding a new earth-centered religion in the midst of a postapocalyptic America.

"You can call it save the world fiction, but it clearly doesn't save anything," she says. "It just calls people's attention to the fact that so much needs to be done and obviously they are people who are running this country who don't care."

Winner of the Hugo Award for science fiction and a MacArthur Genius Fellowship, Butler's fiction bends the boundaries of race and gender, while focusing on the problems of pollution, the legacy of slavery, and racism. *The Independent* spoke with Butler, while she was on tour promoting *Fledgling*, her first novel in nearly a decade.

KAZEMBE BALAGUN: What were some of your major influences in terms of [your] decision to start writing science fiction?

OCTAVIA E. BUTLER: I began reading science fiction before

I was twelve and started writing science fiction around the same time. I was attracted to science fiction because it was so wide-open. I was able to do anything and there were no walls to hem you in and there was no human condition that you were stopped from examining. Well, writing was what I wanted to do, it was always what I wanted to do. I had novels to write so I wrote them.

BALAGUN: You mention wide openness and I noticed in *Lilith's Brood* and your most recent novel *Fledgling*, there [is] a great concern with bending the constraints of gender, race and sexuality, as well as open relationships. Do you think polygamy is the future of humanity?

BUTLER: No, I think the future of humanity will be like the past; we'll do what we've always done and there will still be human beings. Granted, there will always be people doing something different and there are a lot of possibilities. I think my characters [Lauren in *Parable of the Sower* and Shori Matthews in *Fledgling*] have communities that are important in their lives or build communities around themselves.

BALAGUN: Your novels deal with the past, future and present as one. Some have compared it to the concept of Sankofa: "We look to the past to understand the present and prepare for the future." How do you see the concept of Sankofa playing in your work?

BUTLER: Well there's only one novel that remotely deals with that concept and that's *Kindred*. I was trying to make real the emotional reality of slavery. I was trying make people feel more about the data they had learned. I wanted to make the past real and [show] how it scars the present.

BALAGUN: What's interesting to you on the literary scene at the moment?

BUTLER: I've been on the book tour for a few weeks, which means I haven't read anything more difficult than a newspaper [*laughs*] so I can't recommend anything in good conscience. One of my favorite books is *Isaac's Storm* by Erik Larson. It gives us a picture of the great storm that hit Galveston, Texas, and gives us a picture of 1900. Also a book called *T-Rex and the Crater of Doom*, by Walter Alvarez. It's a history of the finding of the asteroid that killed off the dinosaurs. I like it because it shows more about how science is done than most books that you read about the subject. It talks about how the way we think about science can become religious if we are not careful. There were people who were firmly entrenched in the belief that things can only happen one way; they found it difficult that it could happen another way.

BALAGUN: Do you see a tension between writing save the world type of fiction and the artistic impulses of the writer?

BUTLER: No, not at all. I have written books about making the world a better place and how to make humanity more survivable. While *Fledgling* is a different type of book, the Parable series serve as cautionary tales. I wrote the Parable books because of the direction of the country. You can call it save the world fiction, but it clearly doesn't save anything. It just calls people's attention to the fact that so much needs to be done, and obviously they are people who are running this country who don't care. I mean, look at what the Congress is doing in terms of taking money away from every cause that is helping people who aren't very rich. Especially making it harder for people to get an education. Who would want to live in a world where there were fewer educated people?

BALAGUN: We're speaking at [a] time of crisis in the country between the Iraq War and Katrina. As a writer, what makes you hopeful for the future?

BUTLER: At the present, I feel so unhopeful. I recognize we will pay more attention when we have different leadership. I'm not exactly sure where that leadership will come from. But that doesn't mean I think we're all going down the toilet; I just don't see where that hope will come from. I think we need people with stronger ideals than John Kerry or Bill Clinton. I think we need people with more courage and vision. It's a shame we have had people who are so damn weak.

THE LAST INTERVIEW

INTERVIEW BY JEN CHAU FONTÁN
ADDICTED TO RACE
JANUARY 30, 2006

JEN CHAU FONTÁN: Today I have the honor of talking with Octavia Butler, the first African American woman to gain popularity and critical acclaim as a science fiction writer. She describes herself as a fifty-eight-year-old writer who can remember being a ten-year-old writer, and who expects someday to be an eighty-year-old writer. Comfortably asocial, a hermit living in a large city, a pessimist, if not careful, a student, endlessly curious, a feminist, an African American, a former Baptist, and an oil-and-water combination of ambition, laziness, insecurity, certainty, and drive. Today, she has twelve published novels under her belt, the latest one titled *Fledgling*. And her fans hope there will be many more books to come. She's known for exploring subjects not usually addressed in sci-fi, including racial inequity, politics, sexuality, and sexual identity. But to tell you the truth, Octavia, I don't think that books of any genre explore these subjects with the same frequency or complexity that you do.

OCTAVIA E. BUTLER: Thank you.

FONTÁN: Thank you so much for joining us on *Addicted to Race* today.

BUTLER: Well, thanks so much.

FONTÁN: I wanted to start off—actually, I'm sure you've done so many interviews. I wanted to ask you a fun question, if you're willing to indulge me: What is one fun fact about you that no one else probably knows?

BUTLER: Oh, goodness. Well, the problem there is I don't know what other people know about me. Sometimes they know things that aren't so.

FONTÁN: Right.

BUTLER: Gee, I don't know. I don't have an answer for that.

FONTÁN: Okay. I'm sure, I'm sure it probably is hard to tell, since there are so many. I mean, at this point, you type in Octavia Butler into a Google search, and so many different sites come up.

BUTLER: Yeah, I was alarmed at that myself. And most of them are done by other people, of course. So there's my own home page, and then there's everything else.

FONTÁN: Yeah. It's kind of a crazy phenomenon, having all of these tools online; I'm sure that you have fans everywhere, so it's kind of interesting to see that happen and strange to kind of reconcile that . . .

BUTLER: . . . to the degree that I can. As I said, sometimes it's wildly inaccurate, but that's life.

FONTÁN: That is life. Okay. Can you start out by telling us a little bit about *Fledgling*, your latest release, and what led you to write a vampire story?

BUTLER: Well, *Fledgling* is a vampire story. It's about a person who is a vampire as a result of being a member of a different species rather than a vampire as a human being, who just got bitten. She has amnesia because she has been injured very badly, and she is being chased. She doesn't know by whom, but whoever it is has already wiped out two branches of her family and is still trying to reach her. So it's really important that she find out what in the world's going on and who's doing it—and how they can be stopped.

FONTÁN: Right.

BUTLER: So it's essentially an adventure story about a vampire. She also has one unusual aspect. I don't hold to the vampires of Bram Stoker. Nobody does these days. But what I like doing is, what I liked doing when I read a few vampire novels, and I did this in the sense of research, and also because I enjoyed them, was make up my own rules. And I preferred the science fiction vampires. So I accepted part of the vampire background, but they were Eastern European or Mediterranean vampires. Well, my character is the first Black vampire, and she exists as a result of her people wanting to have a twenty-four-hour day, and they really don't like being helpless for about twelve hours out of the day. So what they discover with her, and with her brother, is that one of the secrets to a twenty-four-hour day is melanin. And they do this by way of genetic engineering.

FONTÁN: Right. And to be honest, I'm glad that you strayed from, I mean, I wouldn't expect anything less of you, but I'm glad you strayed from that typical vampire story because you wind up really addressing so many issues surrounding race. And it's interesting that some people who I've talked to about this book, we talk about how Shori, this main character, has to deal with a lot of racism. Some of the families are not accepting of her dark skin and continually argue that she's not full Ina.

BUTLER: Well, Ina is the name of the species that she's a part of. Yes. Your pronunciation was fine. I just wanted to explain who the Ina were.

FONTÁN: Exactly. Thank you for doing that. So they continually argue that she's not full Ina, and it's interesting to see such an American and human concept infiltrate a community like this.

BUTLER: But they've lived among human beings all their existence. And some of them have taken up human prejudices. And I think that's very much what would happen. I remember several years ago there was a dustup in Japan, because for some reason some of the Japanese had taken up an anti-Semitic attitude. I don't mean in any way that it was everybody in Japan or in any way spread completely, but just that some people had taken it up and accepted it as natural.

FONTÁN: Right. And that is something that we assumed that because they were living amongst humans in America, that this was something that was basically going to be played out in their communities as well. But something that was interesting, the interesting twist in *Fledgling*, is that being Black actually has more benefits . . .

BUTLER: For them.

FONTÁN: Yes, exactly. So then the question, I don't think that you could look at it and say, oh, this is a simple case of racism and that they have problems with her because there is this kind of, perhaps this underlying hatred of that, which they couldn't have.

BUTLER: Keep in mind that they also, the ones who were most objecting to her, were people who were old enough to remember slavery and have been part of it in one way or another. They could have been slaveholders. I don't make it clear that they were, but they could have been. So they have come through a time that has shaped their attitudes, and sometimes when people are wronged, when, in this country, for instance, it seems really obvious that Black people are not likely to be forgiving for what was done to them, and this is one of the things that the bigoted ones are suffering from. They maybe have a little bit of the guilt and they don't like to be reminded of it.

FONTÁN: Right. That makes sense. And something that I find so interesting about your books is that there is this kind of made-up element, but then there's also, they're kind of living within dynamics that we're so used to, that exist in our real world.

So can you just talk a little bit about that and what inspires you to create these worlds? A lot of people I've heard of talk about your books and just say, "I have no idea how she comes up with these things." You know, they're so brilliant because they capture so many of the things that we are really dealing with.

BUTLER: Well, the interesting thing about racism and all the other isms is they're never as simple as they sound and I like to go into the complexities, not just what did these people do, but why did they do it? And they don't often know themselves why they did what they did. So, when I wrote *Wild Seed* several years ago, I guess you could call that a vampire story too, but it's not about a blood-drinking vampire. It's about a kind of soul-destroying vampire, Doro; he was really very dangerous. Not only because he considered himself to be above what was going on with everybody else, he did what he did because he could, and also because he kind of needed to. Hurting people, killing people, but also he had, this goes into the other novel more than I want to, he was a little nuts, and there was a good reason for that. He had a problem that I don't give my current vampires; Doro couldn't die.

FONTÁN: Right.

BUTLER: He hadn't been able to find a way to die. Now, I guess I was kind of not really interested in doing another immortal character because my vampires in *Fledgling* are not immortal. They're just, they just live a very long time. They live about five hundred years. But that goes way off into things that you were not talking about. So I'll let you go on.

FONTÁN: Okay. Well, one thing that I wanted to bring up is the theme of mixing that is definitely present in your work, mixing of species—

BUTLER: And certainly in this country.

FONTÁN: Exactly. Well, Octavia, we're on the same page. That's exactly what I wanted to talk to you about. You know, obviously these are trends that are happening in the world. And so through your writing, you're really kind of working through these issues and thinking about these issues. So I just wanted to kind of hear your thoughts on that.

BUTLER: Hmm. Well, bring up another book that I wrote some time ago called *Kindred*. The very name of it is intended to make people think about the way we've lived in this country. And it's always been a matter of mixing, whether it was Native Americans and whites, or Blacks and whites, or Native Americans and Blacks, or whatever. It was always happening. And it was always kind of denied, not looked at. And, or, or even pretended that there was a pretense that it was either impossible or that if it happened, it was very rare. And yet it was always there.

FONTÁN: Yes . . .

BUTLER: And here it is, my, my characters can't interbreed in *Fledgling* because they are a different species. What they get up [to] is, what they get through is, as I mentioned, some genetic engineering. But it still seems very distasteful to one group of the Ina. And human beings don't know about it for the most part, so they don't have an opinion, but if there were, if there was a lot of human knowledge, I'm sure it would be very distasteful to some of the human beings.

FONTÁN: Right. And I'm glad that you bring that up. I mean, it's something that we talk about on *Addicted to Race* all the time, that this mixed identity is not a new one. It's been around for generations. But even though, you know—

BUTLER: It's what human beings do when they come together, whether they're voluntarily or involuntarily.

FONTÁN: Right. And I'm sure you've noticed this too, the way that people talk about it. I mean, just a few years back when, I guess it was with census 2000, that we first had a chance to check more than one racial box. It became, it gained more visibility, and people were just, you know, article after article. Now it's hip to be mixed and look at this, and everybody's mixed. And, you know it's kind of being described as this brand-new identity when in reality [*laugh*], Octavia and I at least know that it's not [*laugh*].

BUTLER: Now, when I was writing *Wild Seed*, I read a book about Louisiana. I can't think of the name of it, but it was from the writer's project done back in the Depression. And it had a long list of what people were called if they were mixed in this way or in that way, or in some other way. And it just went on and on about it, so there were people who were acknowledging it, but I think Louisiana was kind of unique in that way. And it was not necessarily discussing them in a nice way.

FONTÁN: Right, right. And it makes sense, like you were saying, there's been a lot of denial about it, and the history of race mixing in this country has not been a pleasant one. You know, there's a lot of violence and, really, I—

BUTLER: I think in the world really. Yeah. It's often been involuntary, at least in the sense, well, it tended to result from war and rape.

FONTÁN: Right, exactly. Exactly.

BUTLER: And slavery. Right. Not just American slavery, but earlier on.

FONTÁN: Right, exactly. Well, there's definitely, as we could see in *Fledgling*, some of the reactions, as you said, to Shori from one of the families, this kind of a mix of hostility, confusion, and sometimes even fascination around her mixed identity. I think that this is one of the reasons why your books resonate so much with so many mixed individuals. This kind of spectrum of reactions is something that we're very familiar with. So I know that people appreciate that because you're dealing with these issues and really taking a look at the intricacies and bringing to light some of the, not problems, but the difficulties, or challenges, that lay ahead in having our society really figure out what to do with these people that don't fit into our existing classifications.

BUTLER: Oh. Kind of a horrible way to put it. But yeah.

FONTÁN: I mean, really, I've been in so many situations where, as a mixed-race person, people insist on categorization and if you say, I am this and this, that's not acceptable. Okay. But which one, which one are you more of? They're always trying to distill it into one simple answer.

BUTLER: I think human beings are categorizing animals. I mean, in a whole different way. As a writer, I am often asked, okay, what do you write now? Is it science fiction? Is it fantasy? Is it speculative fiction? You know, is it magical realism? And they really are annoyed with me for not sticking a name on my work that covers everything I've ever written. Which is ridiculous.

FONTÁN: It is ridiculous. But I think you're right. No matter what it is, people wanna find the simple term to classify it.

BUTLER: It's an excuse for not thinking.

FONTÁN: Exactly. I totally agree with that. One interesting thing I think that you show through *Fledgling*, also, is that despite the fear of the other, it's very common for these creatures, like Shori, to be beneficial to those with whom they mate or connect to.

BUTLER: It's a symbiotic relationship. So that each is beneficial to the other.

FONTÁN: Right. And so usually the kind of fear that happens in the beginning gives way to acceptance and appreciation of this kind of symbiotic relationship, and an interdependency usually forms from it. So, can you talk a little bit about this, and if you think that this connects in any way to the real-life things?

BUTLER: I think symbiosis has always been something that fascinated me, and this—I'm gonna wander away from race again. I don't know if that bothers you, but I've read a lot of biology, I'm fascinated by it, and I was so happy, I remember, to find Lynn Margulis, a biologist who talks about symbiogenesis, the evolution by symbiosis, by coming together as opposed to evolution by conflict and the strongest wins and that kind of thing. And she was not talking about people. She's talking mainly about microorganisms, but still, it's true, I think with people as well as some animals and microorganisms, on many levels, we wind up being strengthened by what we join, or what joins us, as well as by what we combat.

FONTÁN: Right. And I think I definitely agree with that. And something that we kind of watch when talking about—

BUTLER: It's something that isn't as dramatic as fighting and killing off the competition. So I don't think it gets as much attention as it might. I think it's interesting that Lynn Margulis, a woman, would be one of its strongest proponents.

FONTÁN: Right. But on the flip side, we also don't want to have people believe in that concept of hybrid vigor, which comes up a lot in—

BUTLER: Oh, it's been around for a long time.

FONTÁN: Oh, yes, definitely. And we just talked to an evolutionary biologist, last on our show, who talked about that. And that's another thing that people think: oh my gosh, this is new information that race doesn't have any scientific basis. This is brand new to me. So he talked about those concepts, going back as far as Darwin, so I definitely think that that's a reality that people are also just starting to kind of come to grips with.

BUTLER: Well, maybe some people. But as I said, it's been around for a very long time. I have an old book from back when I was in school, which, believe me, was quite a while ago, and it talks about hybrid vigor and that kind of thing.

FONTÁN: Definitely. I wanted to ask you about your women characters. You show a lot of strong women and not just women, but women of color. And so I wanted to just ask you about the kind of role they were—

BUTLER: They were the people I didn't see when I was growing up. I read omnivorously, I loved to read but I didn't find strong women characters, or at least if I did, and they were rare, they were definitely only white, and it was like the strong women characters of the 1950s. So when they found Mr. Right, they immediately sort of collapsed, as far as their strength was concerned. So I wanted to write about people that I could identify with, could respect, that I would enjoy reading about. And that's what I wound up doing. I wanted to write about people that I saw around me. I had this really strong grandmother who was, if she had been the kind of person who women were portrayed as back during the fifties and earlier, she would've died without issue. I mean, I think a lot of us have these wonderful, strong women in our backgrounds. And why not honor them? Why not write about people like that instead of writing about these poor little wimps, and also I had been reading, I mentioned this earlier, I had been reading a lot of vampire stories. Once I knew I wanted to write one, I read even more. And what I discovered was, over and over again, the most prominent vampires were big, strong men. And the women, even if they were vampires, were poor, weak little things.

FONTÁN: Right.

BUTLER: Or they were evil. So, here we go again. I didn't want—that was the commonplace nonsense, and I didn't want to write that.

FONTÁN: Exactly. And let me tell you, people appreciate that. People really appreciate your writing for those reasons, that you're not going along with the clichés and that you're showing something that does exist in the real world. Strong people of color, strong women of color, but that we don't get to see written about. So, on behalf of all the fans, thank you.

BUTLER: Oh, I think there's a little bit more of it now, but I'm glad to see it; it took a while.

FONTÁN: Definitely. So do you plan on writing a sequel to *Fledgling*? What do you think is coming up next?

BUTLER: I really don't know. I'm getting through some heart problems right now. And the meds that I take kind of leave me so totally washed out that I barely write anything. So I don't know what I'll be doing next, but if it isn't *Fledgling* I definitely have other ideas. I have ideas for at least four other novels, so things will definitely be coming eventually.

FONTÁN: Good. Well, we'll be sending you good thoughts so that you stay nice and strong and continue to do the fabulous work that you're doing.

BUTLER: Thank you.

FONTÁN: You're welcome. One more question. Many people have been wondering where exactly is it that one would be able to meet an Ooloi from *Lilith's Brood*? Everyone, oh my gosh! Octavia, let me tell you, Octavia, I read this book, I met you just recently at the Graduate College of New York.

BUTLER: Oh yes.

FONTÁN: And I told you that my group, which is a group of mixed individuals and interracial couples, that we read *Lilith's Brood*. And it had such a profound effect on so many of us.

And we continue to talk about those characters. And it's so funny 'cause everyone's like, oh, my life would be so much better if I just had one of those.

BUTLER: But doing that was really fun because I had to figure it out before I could write it, you know? And when I grew up, I was reading a lot of science fiction and fantasy and always there were these little bits that would come out, mostly in short stories for some reason, where somebody would say something like, oh, this alien race had twenty-seven different sexes, every single one of which was essential for reproduction. And then they would go on to talk about other things, and we never got to find out what anybody did. And I think I swore to myself then, that if I wrote about races with more than two sexes, I would at least tell what people did and why they were there. I mean, why they worked well with each other. And I think the Ooloi was my first effort in that direction. And again, because people are such categorizing animals, I had a lot of trouble with people who kept saying, oh, the Ooloi is a mix of male and female. Which it isn't in any way at all. But that was the easy way to think about it.

FONTÁN: Exactly.

BUTLER: Because what it is, is a rather complex creature that exists for a different reason altogether. So it was fun figuring it out and it was annoying having people simplify it and make it sound inaccurate.

FONTÁN: Well, it's definitely fun to read about. Well, actually,

I'm glad of that. Yeah. Thank you so much for the time that you've given me tonight. It has been such an honor to talk with you.

BUTLER: Well, thank you. And I hope the program goes well.

FONTÁN: Thank you so much. Everybody go out, make sure you pick up a copy of *Fledgling* by Octavia Butler.

OCTAVIA E. BUTLER was a pioneer of the science fiction genre who received a MacArthur "Genius" Grant and PEN West Lifetime Achievement Award for her body of work. Born in Pasadena in 1947, she was raised by her mother and her grandmother. She was the author of several award-winning novels including *Parable of the Sower* (1993), which was a *New York Times* Notable Book of the Year, and *Parable of the Talents* (1995), winner of the Nebula Award for the best science fiction novel published that year. She was acclaimed for her lean prose, strong protagonists, and social observations in stories that range from the distant past to the far future.

SAMUEL R. DELANY is an American science-fiction novelist and literary critic. He is the recipient of the Kessler Award, four Nebula awards, and two Hugo awards. In 2002, he was inducted into the Science Fiction Hall of Fame, and was named a Grand Master of Science Fiction by the Science Fiction and Fantasy Writers of America in 2013. From 1975 to 2015, he taught at SUNY Buffalo, SUNY Albany, the University of Massachusetts-Amherst, and Temple University. He currently resides in Philadelphia.

JEFFREY ELLIOTT was the editor of legendary science fiction fanzine *Thrust*.

ROSALIE G. HARRISON was an editor and writer for the *Equal Opportunity Forum*.

RANDALL KENAN was the author of the biography *James Baldwin: American Writer*, and the collection of oral histories

Walking on Water: Black American Lives at the Turn of the 21st Century, as well as the novel *A Visitation of Spirits* and the short story collection *Let the Dead Bury Their Dead*. His last work of fiction, *If I Had Two Wings*, was a finalist for the National Book Critics Circle Award, and over his career, his work was awarded numerous honors, including a Guggenheim Fellowship, a Whiting Writers Award, the Sherwood Anderson Award, the John Dos Passos Award, the Rome Prize from the American Academy of Arts and Letters, and numerous other prizes.

TERRY GROSS was born and raised in Brooklyn and received a bachelor's degree in English and M.Ed. in communications from the State University of New York at Buffalo. She has been the host of NPR's *Fresh Air* for over three decades and is the author of *All I Did Was Ask: Conversations with Writers, Actors, Musicians, and Artists*. Gross was recognized with the Columbia Journalism Award from Columbia University's Graduate School of Journalism in 2008 and an Honorary Doctor of Humanities degree from Princeton University in 2002.

STEPHEN W. POTTS received his doctorate from the University of California at Berkeley. He has taught courses on science fiction, fantasy, film, and other popular genres, on creative writing, and on youth culture for both the Literature and Communication departments. He is also creator and editor of Armageddon Buffet, an online journal of fiction and commentary.

CECILIA TAN is the founder of Circlet Press, publishers of erotic science fiction and fantasy, and the author of short story collections *Black Feathers*, and *White Flames*. Her short stories in *Ms. Magazine*, *Asimov's Science Fiction*, *Absolute Magnitude*, and *Strange Horizons*.

DARRELL SCHWEITZER is an author, literary critic, and the editor of many anthologies of speculative fiction and dark fantasy. He was nominated for the World Fantasy Best Collections Award in 2000 for *Necromancies and Netherworlds*.

JOSHUNDA SANDERS is an author and executive communications leader. She is the author of the children's book *I Can Write the World*, the journalism textbook *How Racism and Sexism Killed Traditional Media: Why the Future of Journalism Depends on Women and People of Color*, and a memoir, *The Beautiful Darkness: A Handbook for Orphans*. In 2018, she was awarded the Bronx Recognizes Its Own (BRIO) Award for excellence in fiction. Her forthcoming novel, *Women of the Post*, is scheduled for publication in summer 2023.

KAZEMBE BALAGUN was born in Harlem and received his B.A. in Philosophy from Hunter College. A writer and cultural historian currently based in the Bronx, he is a frequent contributor to the radical journal *The Indypendent*.

JENNIFER CHAU FONTÀN is a somatic leadership coach and was a co-creator and co-host of the podcast *Addicted to Race*. In addition to her twenty-plus years working toward racial equity inside and alongside progressive sector nonprofits, she has been an organizer of communities for multiracial individuals, interracial couples, and mixed families through her work with Swirl. She has also shared her perspective on race and racism in media outlets including *The New York Times*, *USA Today*, *The San Francisco Chronicle*, CNN, and National Public Radio.

THE LAST INTERVIEW SERIES

OCTAVIA E. BUTLER:
THE LAST INTERVIEW

$19.99 / $25.99 CAN

978-1-68589-105-3
ebook: 978-1-68589-106-0

bell hooks:
THE LAST INTERVIEW

$18.99 / $24.99 CAN

978-1-68589-079-7
ebook: 978-1-68589-080-3

KURT COBAIN:
THE LAST INTERVIEW

$17.99 / $23.99 CAN

978-1-68589-009-4
ebook: 978-1-68589-010-0

DIEGO MARADONA:
THE LAST INTERVIEW

$17.99 / $23.99 CAN

978-1-61219-973-3
ebook: 978-1-61219-974-0

JOAN DIDION:
THE LAST INTERVIEW

$17.99 / $23.99 CAN

978-1-68589-011-7
ebook: 978-1-68589-012-4

JANET MALCOLM:
THE LAST INTERVIEW

$17.99 / $23.99 CAN

978-1-61219-968-9
ebook: 978-1-68589-012-4

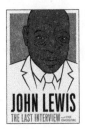

JOHN LEWIS:
THE LAST INTERVIEW

$16.99 / $22.99 CAN

978-1-61219-962-7
ebook: 978-1-61219-963-4

FRIDA KAHLO:
THE LAST INTERVIEW

$16.99 / $22.99 CAN

978-1-61219-875-0
ebook: 978-1-61219-876-7

THE LAST INTERVIEW SERIES

**FRED ROGERS:
THE LAST INTERVIEW**

$16.99 / $21.99 CAN

978-1-61219-895-8
ebook: 978-1-61219-896-5

**TONI MORRISON:
THE LAST INTERVIEW**

$16.99 / $22.99 CAN

978-1-61219-873-6
ebook: 978-1-61219-874-3

**SHIRLEY CHISHOLM:
THE LAST INTERVIEW**

$16.99 / $22.99 CAN

978-1-61219-897-2
ebook: 978-1-61219-898-9

**GRAHAM GREENE:
THE LAST INTERVIEW**

$16.99 / $22.99 CAN

978-1-61219-814-9
ebook: 978-1-61219-815-6

**RUTH BADER GINSBURG:
THE LAST INTERVIEW**

$17.99 / $23.99 CAN

978-1-61219-919-1
ebook: 978-1-61219-920-7

**URSULA K. LE GUIN:
THE LAST INTERVIEW**

$16.99 / $21.99 CAN

978-1-61219-779-1
ebook: 978-1-61219-780-7

**JULIA CHILD:
THE LAST INTERVIEW**

$16.99 / $22.99 CAN

978-1-61219-733-3
ebook: 978-1-61219-734-0

**ROBERTO BOLAÑO:
THE LAST INTERVIEW**

$15.95 / $17.95 CAN

978-1-61219-095-2
ebook: 978-1-61219-033-4

THE LAST INTERVIEW SERIES

**KURT VONNEGUT:
THE LAST INTERVIEW**

$15.95 / $17.95 CAN

978-1-61219-090-7
ebook: 978-1-61219-091-4

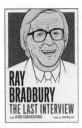

**RAY BRADBURY:
THE LAST INTERVIEW**

$15.95 / $15.95 CAN

978-1-61219-421-9
ebook: 978-1-61219-422-6

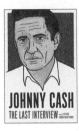

**JOHNNY CASH:
THE LAST INTERVIEW**

$16.99 / $22.99 CAN

978-1-61219-893-4
ebook: 978-1-61219-894-1

**JAMES BALDWIN:
THE LAST INTERVIEW**

$16.99 / $22.99 CAN

978-1-61219-400-4
ebook: 978-1-61219-401-1

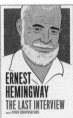

**MARILYN MONROE:
THE LAST INTERVIEW**

$16.99 / $22.99 CAN

978-1-61219-877-4
ebook: 978-1-61219-878-1

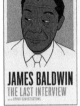

**GABRIEL GARCÍA
MÁRQUEZ: THE LAST
INTERVIEW**

$15.95 / $15.95 CAN

978-1-61219-480-6
ebook: 978-1-61219-481-3

**ERNEST HEMINGWAY:
THE LAST INTERVIEW**

$15.95 / $20.95 CAN

978-1-61219-522-3
ebook: 978-1-61219-523-0

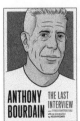

**ANTHONY BOURDAIN:
THE LAST INTERVIEW**

$17.99 / $23.99 CAN

978-1-61219-824-8
ebook: 978-1-61219-825-5

THE LAST INTERVIEW SERIES

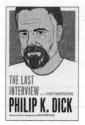

PHILIP K. DICK:
THE LAST INTERVIEW

$15.95 / $20.95 CAN

978-1-61219-526-1
ebook: 978-1-61219-527-8

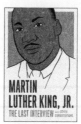

MARTIN LUTHER KING, JR.:
THE LAST INTERVIEW

$15.99 / $21.99 CAN

978-1-61219-616-9
ebook: 978-1-61219-617-6

NORA EPHRON:
THE LAST INTERVIEW

$15.95 / $20.95 CAN

978-1-61219-524-7
ebook: 978-1-61219-525-4

CHRISTOPHER HITCHENS:
THE LAST INTERVIEW

$15.99 / $20.99 CAN

978-1-61219-672-5
ebook: 978-1-61219-673-2

DAVID BOWIE:
THE LAST INTERVIEW

$16.99 / $22.99 CAN

978-1-61219-575-9
ebook: 978-1-61219-576-6

HUNTER S. THOMPSON:
THE LAST INTERVIEW

$15.99 / $20.99 CAN

978-1-61219-693-0
ebook: 978-1-61219-694-7

BILLIE HOLIDAY:
THE LAST INTERVIEW

$16.99 / $22.99 CAN

978-1-61219-674-9
ebook: 978-1-61219-675-6

KATHY ACKER:
THE LAST INTERVIEW

$16.99 / $21.99 CAN

978-1-61219-731-9
ebook: 978-1-61219-732-6